APPARITIONS, AEROBICS, AND ARSON

BEWITCHER'S BEACH PARANORMAL COZY
MYSTERIES

BOOK 3

EMILY FLUKE

ALSO BY EMILY FLUKE

Be sure to snag the prequels to both the Mari Fable Mysteries, and the Bewitcher's Beach Paranormal Cozy Mysteries FREE from my newsletter: The Glass Coffin and Be Careful What You Witch For.

https://landing.mailerlite.com/webforms/landing/y4h6c8

For everyone who invites friends into their homes for the holidays. Thank you for being someone's found family.

Oyster Inn

Pet Grooming

Hair Salon

Coffee Shop

Fire House

Soccer Field

Roller Rink & Diner

Clinic

Art Studio

Seashell Shop

Clothing Shop

Sunglasses Shop

Office Building

Beach

CAST OF CHARACTERS

Noema Wolf (temporary last name. Once werewolves are turned they have no memory of their previous life):

As a werewolf who can smell emotions and a lover of mystery movies, Noema finds herself sniffing out suspects whenever a troublesome visitor upsets her cozy, seaside town. But another case is not what this single mother of four, manager of Mockbuster Video Rental, and playwright needs thrown into her busy schedule.

Halen, Dio, Jovi, and Stevie Wolf:

These four mischievous 'pups' each help their mom solve mysteries or run the video rental shop in their own unique ways. As born werewolves, they don't experience memory loss —but as eight-year-olds, they suffer selective hearing when it comes to following the rules.

Sheriff Sett Lawrence:

This overprotective gargoyle takes life too seriously. His six foot, six inch stony, body with muscular wings and horns, does nothing to match his introverted, patient, and studious personality. But it certainly frightens visitors.

Crow:

A mysterious man with a handsome smirk. Crow took advantage of the low housing market in Bewitcher's Beach after a newcomer was recently murdered. This "tall dark" has plenty of secrets but isn't afraid to tease, flirt, and joke in the face of danger. And as hidden as he may seem—as the new owner of Roller Shakes—Crow socializes with the whole town on a regular basis.

Mae Wildefyre:

Like her husband, Wallace, and other half-dragons, Mae resembles a human but has shiny, scaly skin. Before, when human hunters came after supernatural people, Mae hid with the other half-dragons, shifting herself to appear fully human. Now, she's the center of attention, and she loves it...until her secrets spread like wildfire.

Hattie Sharpe:

This harsh, flapper-girl starlet became a ghost in the height of the Roaring Twenties when her bold attitude landed her the target of a deadly Hollywood stunt. Now, she directs Everland Theater's plays and tells it like it is, no matter how many enemies it creates.

Bette Sharpe:

Hattie's teenage daughter. This ghost babysits the wolf kids for money to develop the film on her Kodak camera. What crime will her photograph's capture?

Mayor Fitz Feet:

As if summoned by his name, this short, shiny-headed mayor and volunteer police officer always appears with a cheerful countenance and a glass-half-full attitude. A leader of a town full of rumors, superstitions, and supernatural creatures must stay positive—even when a murder threatens to ruin Bewitcher's Beach's reputation. And his.

Miss Raven:

Retired reaper and owner of Aerobics Alive, the best (and only) exercise studio in Bewitcher's Beach. She fills her clientele up with donuts so they'll return to burn off the extra calories. "A workout a day keeps the reaper away!"

Zed and Reed:

Father and son contractors. Visiting Bewitcher's Beach to remodel homes. Oh, and the teenage Reed may or may not have heart eyes for a certain teenage ghost.

Cliff Conflick:

The unstable apparition of a murdered plastic surgeon. This ghost was a jerk in real life and is even angrier in death. But he's not descended into a poltergeist. Does that make him more or less dangerous?

Squeaks:

A mouse. Arrogant, intelligent, and adorable, but still just a mouse.

CHAPTER 1
YULE BE SORRY

I KICKED off my neon blue sneakers and stretched the thick socks over my crossed ankles, settling in to watch the robber get handcuffed. At the wrath of a clever child, the robber suffered a burned head and crispy, flaming hat that sparked a laugh from me. The movie *Home Alone* was an instant favorite for me and my four kids. The giggles that echoed from the theater's front row proved their love for it. Since we could watch it a hundred times and still laugh, it was deemed our new holiday tradition.

Thanks to a donated projector and a jerry-rigged VCR set up on the stage at Everland Theater, we invited half the town to our Christmas movie nights. We didn't have relatives of our own—that we knew of—but we created a little family after settling in Bewitcher's Beach. And as the resident movie buff and owner of Mockbuster video rental, I felt it was my duty to bring the joy of an entertaining comedy or spooky mystery to the locals.

"We should have more movie nights. This was a brilliant idea, Noema," the ghost floating in the seat beside me said.

"Why, thank you." I grinned at my best friend, but she was busy gaping at the actors and actresses displayed across the stage's curtain. Hattie became a ghost during her years as a starlet in 1920s Hollywood and, though she longed to return, she fit best here with the dense population of supernatural people. Bewitcher's Beach was full of people like us. Only a few peculiarities distinguished us from humans, like the wolf ears that jutted from my curly hair or the slight transparent sheen of Hattie's ghostly manifestation.

"I feel like I'm at a real movie theater." Hattie's sapphire eyes sparkled brighter than the costume jewelry she haunted. The shine behind her gaze matched her golden flapper-girl dress. "I really needed this. Does everyone get depressed when holidays end, or is it just me? Christmas can't come soon enough."

I tossed my thumb over my shoulder at the handsome reaper who sat in the chair on my other side. "I can't take all the credit. Crow was the one who got the VCR working and connected to the projector."

Giggles erupted from the front row again. The kids wiggled and pointed at the screen as the two movie bandits bickered their way to the cop car.

A hand wrapped around mine, and I looked up at Crow. He flashed me a sideways smile exaggerated by the hooked scar on his cheek. The combination of dark curls and eyes that gleamed with mischief made him dangerously handsome. After a murderer tried to kill us both only weeks before, we agreed to keep it casual—even if being exclusive could mean happiness in the face of homicide. Though we'd decided to take dating slowly, his look sent a thrill through me that suggested otherwise. I offered my hand and interlaced my fingers through his, smiling back.

The credits rolled, blaring a familiar Christmas song. The kids cheered and hopped onto the stage where the projector displayed the rolling credits against the red curtain. The kids mimicked the ending scene of *Home Alone*, pretending to serve justice like the character in the movie did to the robbers who invaded his home.

My pack of four eight-year-olds loved the classic Christmas heist because they fancied themselves mini detectives after witnessing me solve crimes that sullied our little community. As a werewolf, I was gifted—or cursed—with the ability to smell people's emotions. That gift often wrapped me up in the hunt for criminals because I could sniff out who was lying.

"I wish solving crimes was that easy," I said, nodding at the movie.

"Right?" Crow said. "Life would be so chill, and we wouldn't even need the protection spell." If only we could find out who tampered with the protection spell that once kept our town safe from criminals like the bandits in *Home Alone,* then true justice could be served. Now, we were exposed to crime.

A jolly rendition of "We Wish You a Merry Christmas" accompanied the movie credits. As the song wrapped up, people slowly got to their feet, stretching and yawning. With holiday music blaring, all I could think about was wrapping presents, Christmas shopping, decorating, and a dozen other ticks on my to-do list. Good thing we started traditions early.

Crow leaned over the arm rest between us and nudged me with his elbow. The scythe-shaped scar across his cheek hooked deeper into his skin with his rakish smirk. "So, are we going to the step aerobics class tomorrow like we promised Mae?" He lifted his chin, and his gaze shifted to the elderly half-dragon woman who stood in the row behind us. The only evidence of her dragon heritage was revealed by a shimmering hint of scales beneath her skin. She spied us looking at her and adjusted the fluffy poodle in her arms, lifting the dog's delicate paw to give us a little wave. The poodle yipped and nipped at her long fingernails but she only chuckled and petted the ferocious little beast.

A puff of air escaped me. "I mean, I promised, and I always keep a promise."

"But are we actually going to make it to the early class this time?"

I frowned. "Oof. Ask me again after tomorrow morning's Diet Pepsi." He laughed, but Diet Pepsi for breakfast wasn't a joke. I enjoyed it every morning with a bite of bacon and eggs. I leaned over to grab my shoes, not wanting to tug them back on since I'd been in neon spandex and sneakers all day. I never made it to the step aerobics class, but at least the intent was there.

Eavesdropping as always, Mae interjected, wagging her finger at us. "I expect to see you two in Miss Raven's studio first thing tomorrow morning! Let's get the jitters out before our long drive."

"It's on my schedule," I said, suppressing a groan at the "bright and early" bit. Mae swore step aerobics was the best form of exercise for a healthy heart. And with as much buttery, salt-soaked popcorn I consumed, I needed it. Plus, a little exercise before our road trip was exactly what my restless legs called for.

After the school bell rang tomorrow afternoon, the pups, Mae, her husband Wallace, and I were to pile into my Astro van and drive the two hours to Shadowvale University, where witches and warlocks studied magic and spells. Spells like the magic that once protected Bewitcher's Beach. Sure, the kids would miss the last week of school, but we had an entire Christmas tour planned. Stopping along the way, we'd visit Mae and Wallace's relatives, build gingerbread houses at a popular bakery, view Christmas lights, and go on a winter hike.

She continued, "You'll have to bring a water bottle, but the studio provides the rest."

"The rest?" Crow asked.

"Dumbbells, trampolines, the step platforms—"

"Trampolines?" I didn't mean to interrupt her, but my ears perked and delicious whiffs of banana cream pie prodded the word to slip out. My excitement smelled heavenly as it buzzed in my chest. "Bouncing sounds fun. Count me in."

"Count me out," Crow grumbled.

"Not a chance." I spun around and mimicked Mae's finger wagging.

He smirked as we stood and shuffled out of the aisle. We paused to mingle in the middle walkway with Mae and her husband as well as Hattie. Wonderful aromas emanated from the joy and contentment everyone finally enjoyed now that two recent murder investigations were concluded and in the past.

In a low voice, Crow said only to me, "I was kidding. If you want me to be at that class tomorrow, I'll be there. How about we call it a date? You can catch me when I fall off the trampoline."

I bit my lip to keep from grinning like a goof. He was willing to try it for me? "Count me in. Again. But I won't be catching anybody since I'll already be on the ground." Yikes. Did I really want to embarrass myself in front of half the town?

I glanced around. Beyond our circle of friends was a variety of people, human and supernatural, young and old, mostly all friendly. Still, the amount was intimidating. Aerobics Alive's classes were packed, and I wasn't known for my coordination.

"It's a date." Crow reached out and tucked a curl behind my ear. For a moment, the dozens of people mingling around us slipped away. He smelled of rainstorms and whiskey. Adventure. "I can't wait to be on the ground next to you."

I laughed, and Mae interjected. "So," she said, "about the Christmas traditions—"

"Shh!" I shushed her and peeked at the kids. "I'm trying to keep the cookie decorating party a surprise. This is the first time the kids get to have a grandma for the holidays." Once a werewolf turned, we could not remember life before. In that process, I lost contact with any family I may have had. And when my husband passed years ago, we were down to just the five of us. This year, thanks to Bewitcher's Beach, we'd start a heap of new traditions with the friends my kids deemed their adopted grandparents.

"Grand*mae*," Mae corrected. "Grandma sounds too old. I'm plenty spry. You'll see how much energy I still have at step aerobics tomorrow." A bit of red sparkled in her eyes, evidence of her half-dragon side. "Good thing too. With all this Christmas baking, I'll be two hundred pounds of sugar cookie."

"Excellent point," I said, patting my stomach. "I'm ready to stuff my face with every Christmas-themed food I can find."

"Really?" Crow waggled his eyebrows at me. "What if I told you I have a surprise of my own? A little holiday flair to Roller Shakes's menu." As the owner of the local roller rink, Crow controlled the in-house diner's menu, which was mostly burgers and fries. With Christmas around the corner, maybe he'd added peppermint milkshakes or cranberry and turkey sandwiches.

"As I was saying." Mae shot Crow a pointed glare. She was a fan of his, just not as my date. "I'm just happy we're leaving town for Christmas." Her smile suddenly twisted and her hand shook as she petted the poodle's head faster and with more pressure. The smell of ammonia filled the air, signaling fear. "In case anything happens here, you know?"

I unlaced my fingers from Crow's hand and gently touched Mae's arm. "What do you mean? Is everything okay?"

Mae's eyes danced around the room before she stepped closer and lowered her voice. "You know how I report for the newspaper?"

"The gossip column, yeah."

She straightened and lifted her chin. "It's more than a gossip column. It informs people of the goings on in Bewitcher's Beach. For their own safety. Like how I've warned everyone that the ghost of Cliff Conflick has taken to harassing and bad-mouthing the town. It helped you avoid him, did it not?"

"It did. You're right," I said. "Cliff's not my biggest fan." The ghost whose murder I'd helped solve didn't exactly thank me for the service. Instead, he heckled me for loving Bewitcher's Beach, calling me tasteless and pathetic. He was just angry that his spirit was tethered to a small town and took it out on anyone who blatantly enjoyed it. "I'm sorry."

She stroked the dog's head quicker as if ramping up to share nail-biting news. "In my research for tomorrow's column, I found out that people right here in Bewitcher's Beach have received threats."

"Threats?" My wolf ears tucked back. Ice chilled my veins. Who wanted to harm our home now? And did the sheriff know? With a peek over my shoulder, I spotted the towering gargoyle cop giving my kids high fives after they finished a convincing performance of *Home Alone* on the stage.

Mae slapped her free hand to her chest and nodded. "Yes, threats. Both the librarian and the new deputy found notes nailed to their doors."

"What did the notes say?" Crow asked.

Wallace, Mae's husband, stepped in. Mae wasn't exactly speaking quietly anymore, and I noticed Hattie and her daughter Bette were also listening. "Something along the lines of 'abandon the premises for your own safety. Vacate Bewitcher's Beach and you'll be spared.'"

The iciness in my veins froze just as my heart sped up. "Could it be a prank?"

Mae frowned. "We thought the same at first because somebody spray painted targets on the deputy's place. But..." Her gaze slid to the sheriff.

Heavy footsteps came up behind me. With Sett came the smell of sourdough bread he baked. You'd never guess the six and a half foot stony officer wore an apron in his free time.

He took a deep breath as if readying for a speech, and everyone in the circle gave him their attention. "Unfortunately, we can't treat it as a prank. Not with the protection spell down and the station understaffed. I'm alone, and on twenty-four-seven duty since Mayor Fitz isn't volunteering as an officer anymore. We can't be too careful." If any phrase described Sett, it was that one. *Can't be too careful* may as well be tattooed on his forehead.

His slate eyes landed on me, and my pulse skipped. I looked away. I was on a date now. With *Crow*.

He continued, "I suspect the vandalism was a warning, so I'm keeping an eye on things. But please, if you hear or see anything odd, give me a call." He was still only looking at me. *Give me a call*. My breath caught, pulse dancing erratically. I would not be giving him a call because we were nothing more than friends. Unless, of course, I sniffed out something fishy regarding those threats. Hopefully I wouldn't. Hopefully they'd amount to nothing and the Christmas season was free of fear and full of cheer.

A bit of smoke emitted from Mae's nose with a heavy breath. Another reminder of her half-dragon side other than the faint shimmer of her skin and tinted red eyes. "My poor baby is nervous with everything going on. She never got a rash like this when we had the protection spell." She hugged her poodle tighter. The dog's beady black eyes bulged, but it wasn't the pet whose nerves I could smell. Mae hid it well, but news of threats against Judy and the deputy rattled her. Likely because she was the landlord for both of their residences.

I gave the poodle a scratch behind the ears as I met Mae's gaze. "It'll be okay. Sett's on it." Of course, real life wasn't a Christmas movie, and crime didn't wrap up with a neat little bow like *Home Alone* suggested. But after a few minutes of gossip and arranging plans, the earlier buzz of nervous energy melted away, and we dispersed. Mae and her husband hurried off to sleep so she could be the first to arrive for Miss Raven's class in the morning, and the ghosts vanished to the attic above the theater. After Sett left, I gave Crow a quick kiss on the cheek, and shut the doors behind him. We rarely locked the theater, but tonight I twisted the lock to seal both doors.

I blew out a breath, expelling all worry away before spinning on my heels. When I called for my kids to get to bed, they moaned and groaned but trudged their way to the back door that shared a wall with Mockbuster. I followed them inside the dark video rental shop and to the stairs that led to our cozy apartment above the shop.

As we said goodnight, I did everything I could not to spill the beans about upcoming Christmas surprises. Hopefully those who received threats wouldn't get a surprise of their own.

CHAPTER 2
NO PLACE
LIKE HOME

THE NEXT MORNING, I dragged myself into Mockbuster after dropping the kids off at school. A yawn over-took me and the door fell shut behind me. I'd given in to the temptation to stay up too late, snacking on popcorn and jotting down screenplay ideas. Out of the dozen ideas, I only half-liked one about fairy tales coming alive.

Trudging up the stairs to the loft, I swapped my robe and slippers for spandex and sneakers. I pulled a purple Roller Shakes hoodie over my head for the chilly walk.

Dressed now, I shuffled into the kitchen. Our two bedroom loft's modest kitchen connected to an even smaller family room. We crammed an old floral-patterned sofa that was as plush as it was pastel in the space with a thrifted coffee table where we ate most of our dinners since the five of us didn't fit the 1950s vinyl kitchen table. I plopped into one of the squeaky chairs and rubbed my eyes. Popping open a can of Diet Pepsi, I prayed the caffeine would give me a boost. I squinted at the green-lit clock on the stove. Half past seven was too early for this time of year when dawn came late and fog often coated the coast for most of the day. But we'd already put the Christmas tree up, and the colorful glow of lights shined into the kitchen from the living room, already brightening my day.

I grabbed a wreath and the hook to hang it from where it was slung over the back of a kitchen chair. I intended to decorate for Christmas before the movie yesterday, but time got away from me. A big red bow hung from the bottom of the wreath. Wrinkles crumpled the velvet fabric, but it was as cheerful as ever.

A little chirp announced our pet mouse's entrance. The tiny zebra mouse skittered into the kitchen and stopped to stand on his hind legs, whiskers and nose twitching until I scooped Squeaks up and slipped him into the big pocket on the front of my hoodie.

With Pepsi in one hand and the wreath in the other, I hurried downstairs. If I didn't get my butt moving, I'd be late for the date with Crow. I needed at least an extra thirty minutes to pop next door and run the screenplay idea past Hattie. She'd bear the truth. Pass or fail on the fairy-tales-come-true premise.

Downstairs was dark without the constant shine of Christmas lights. As I walked past the rows of VHS tapes, the wall of candy, and the register to the right, I swore to decorate the shop before the day was over. Starting with the wreath. I headed for the glass door when a flutter caught my eye.

Wind tossed a paper that was pasted on the outside of the door. Odd. Sometimes I posted a change in hours or a sign about auditions for Everland Theater's plays, but I hadn't put anything on the door in weeks.

The bell above the door chimed when I yanked it open. Another briny gust of wind sent the paper flapping until I pinched it and tugged, peeling the tape at the top off the glass. My eyes flew across the note as my heart plunged into my stomach.

Noema Wolf, abandon the premises. Vacate Bewitcher's Beach and Mockbuster will be spared.

"Oh no..." The breeze swept my voice away. They're threatening me now too? Who'd left this? My skin prickled where the tip of my ponytail brushed the back of my neck, and shivers spread through me. I swallowed a little gasp and spun around. The cobblestone street was empty. I scanned the town beyond the street to be sure everyone out on this early Friday morning was friends—not foe.

Bewitcher's Beach was quiet except for the rhythmic lap of the salty waves in the distance. Only a few steps from Mockbuster's front door, I could see a few of the businesses that lined the main street throughout town. The cobblestone surrounded a football-sized field of green grass where winding pathways cut through and black iron lamp posts scattered to brighten the park. Fog misting the morning air blocked my view of the far side of town.

And the person who left the threat was nowhere to be seen.

Everything was as it should be. For now. Why did someone want Mockbuster empty? What would they do to our home? I crumpled the note in my hand and scanned the town again.

Shops glittered with Christmas lights in every hue, except for Chanel's Boutique. The siren's chic clothing store that was all class and no color was the only building to decorate with simple white lights. Other businesses matched their decorations to their bright coloring. The green and cream of Oyster Inn, the blue and red barber pole outside Shaggy's Hair Salon, the yellow door of Triton's Taffy shop beside the workout studio, and the studio itself that was stuck in the 1980s with orange and magenta walls visible through the giant front window.

Nothing matched and the buildings were old, but I wouldn't change anything about Bewitcher's Beach. It was the happiest place on earth—for me, anyway. For now. What if we came back from the road trip to a ransacked home? Or stolen VHS tapes from the shop? They started with spray painting, but did it end there? I couldn't bear to cancel the road trip, our holiday plans, but to leave Mockbuster exposed...

A sudden chill descended upon me. I nearly jumped out of my skin when an icy ghost swept by.

Hattie floated from Everland Theater, chasing after her teenage daughter. The two ghosts argued loud enough for half the town to hear. "No. I forbid you from meeting up with that *goon*. The kid smokes cigarettes and flaunts tattoos and has hair like a dinosaur!" She waved her arms wildly.

"Mom!" Bette whined as she came to a stop and spun around, surging toward her mother. "You smoked cigarettes when you were alive—"

"It was the Roaring Twenties, darling, everyone smoked," Hattie said. When she spotted me, her brows scrunched beneath her pearl headband and a smile curled half her mouth. She hurried to my side, the icy chill of her ghostly fingers passing through my arm. "How about this, Bette? I will interview the boy with Noema present so she can smell if he's a liar or sneaky or anything untoward. If I deem him worthy, then and only then can you spend time with him."

Sneaky? Another shiver shuddered down my spine, and I fingered the threatening note in my pocket.

"Mom!" Bette frowned at me.

It was times like these I considered my ability a curse. Sniffing out lies for a friend? Uncomfortable. Not my favorite way to help people, that was for sure.

I stepped away from Hattie but stayed quiet, wanting to support my best friend in her parenting but also not wanting to get involved. It didn't matter, because Bette surged away and Hattie followed, leaving me behind.

I blew out a breath. I'd love to get Hattie's thoughts on the note, not to mention the screenplay, but now was clearly not the time. Still, I wanted to share the weight of this threat so I wasn't alone with it hovering over me like a dark rain cloud.

The image of a stony gargoyle clad in a blue uniform popped into my mind. Sett would want to know I'd received a threat. If I was lucky, he'd offer information about the other notes and give me insight on who wanted to frighten me. And why.

I quickly placed the hook over the top of the door and hung the wreath so that the little burst of red and green cheer replaced the creepy note. I folded the paper and tucked it beside Squeaks in my front pocket then headed straight for the grassy grounds. Crossing through the park was a shortcut to the police station on the other side of town. Sett was sure to be there already, considering he was short-staffed and working overtime. A drop of relief washed through me. I didn't want to be alone with this loaded note much longer.

Squeaks stirred in my pocket, chirping and restless as if he could hear my thoughts. I patted his head through the fabric. "I know, I'm not alone. I have my brave little mouse." With that, he relaxed again.

But I didn't.

Two figures lurked at the edge of the park. The morning was still too dim and foggy to make out who they were. Did the person who left the note plan to follow me? My hackles raised and fingernails slowly grew into wolf's claws. Sharp canines extended from my teeth, and I was ready to shift into my defensive wolf form until I recognized a familiar laugh. As quickly as they came, my claws and fangs receded.

It was only Mae.

The elderly half-dragon and her husband strolled by with their yappy poodle nipping at its leash. Wallace was dressed in a soft bathrobe without a care in the world while Mae scurried ahead of him holding a pair of brightly colored dumbbells. She spotted me, raising one of the dumbbells above her head with a wave. "Noema!" Bustling closer, she stopped in front of me with a huff. "I won't keep you from getting breakfast." She glanced at Roller Shakes, assuming that was where I was headed. "And we want to get to class early. But I have to tell you what Wallace and I were discussing after we left last night." She sucked in a breath and gently laid a hand on my arm. "Honey, we're not so sure now is a good time to go on the Christmas trip with you and the pups. Judy and the deputy both rent their cottages from me. With my rentals under threat of vandalism and the clean up from the graffiti—" Another pause. Her brow bunched, and it was my turn to lay my other hand on hers.

"I understand." Though it hurt. But not as badly as it would hurt the kids. Which, in turn, would break my heart all over again. To leave their new grandparents, just when we finally had family, blood-related or not, gutted me. I chewed at my lip, and Mae buried me in a hug.

"I don't want to upset the little ones," she said, pulling back. "What if we move all our Christmas activities to Bewitcher's Beach?"

Postpone the road trip? No... At Shadowvale, I hoped to learn more about myself and our extended family from the history of a spell book. Buried in the powerful grimoire, a prophecy hinted at a werewolf like me, but since I wasn't a witch, I needed the help of the university's students and professors to make sense of it. And when a magical mark appeared on my collarbone, tying me back to that same grimoire, I had another clue that gave me hope. Hope that I was somehow related to the creator of the spells and whoever had penned the prophecy itself. If I was, we'd finally have a relative. We'd finally know our family.

But Mae and Wallace were our family now. They were right here in front of me, loving my kids, planning holiday cheer, giving hugs. As much as I wanted to visit Shadowvale and get answers, the family I'd found here was more important. Plus, this vandalism had to be dealt with—or prevented. "You know what? The kids really shouldn't miss school anyway. If you're both staying, so are we."

Mae's eyes lit up, and she lifted both dumbbells into the air. "Well, isn't that just the best news I've heard all week? Did you hear that, Wallace? My kitchen is bigger than my sister's anyway, so cookie decorating will fit all the pups much easier." Giddy now, she hurried off to catch up with Wallace and Babette. They both disappeared inside the studio, though I guessed Wallace wasn't there to exercise, but for the donuts Miss Raven put out to keep customers returning to burn off the sugar.

I grinned. Until a gust of wind howled. The draft blew between a boutique and a saltwater taffy shop, ominous and the only noise on the empty street.

I was alone again.

My hair tickled the back of my neck, and I scratched at it as I marched forward, chin up. I refused to be intimidated. Even so, I tuned into the surrounding sounds as a precaution. In my human form, my wolf ears never changed, always furry and sticking out at the top of my head around my curly dark hair. I kept them perked and pricked for any odd noise, alert—but not intimidated.

That didn't mean I couldn't hurry to the station. I cupped one hand under the mouse in my pocket and took off into a jog past a foggy outdoor ice skating rink. The small patch of ice butted up to a wooden stage that was as temporary as the rink, only built in preparation for the mayoral speeches.

Once the station came into view, I slowed and apologized for bouncing Squeaks. Inside, Sett was stooped over paperwork on his desk. He rested his chin on his fist and didn't look up when I came in. The station was nothing more than two closets, one for storage and the other transformed into an interrogation room, a half kitchen, a bathroom, and a jail cell. Sett's massive desk split the front room into half. Beyond that, a narrow hallway led to where criminals were kept.

The cozy space was made tighter with the Christmas decorations. Along the right wall, Sett had transformed the top of the filing cabinets into a miniature light-up version of Bewitcher's Beach. But this ceramic version of town had snow coating everything, blanketing it in seasonal serenity.

A chirp startled me from the soothing scene.

Squeaks lived up to his namesake. He chirped at the smell of coffee. A rich and nutty aroma wafted from the pot at the little kitchen counter on the left. My mouse thought himself a very distinguished gentleman and insisted on sipping coffee and tea. Even wine on occasion.

Sett startled, blinking at me as he sat upright. His sharply angled brows lost their edge, and his tense jaw melted into relaxation. I thought I caught a lift at the edge of his lips, but Sett didn't smile. He stood and headed for the mini refrigerator beneath the kitchen counter.

"Morning, Noema. Would you like a drink?" He crouched and opened the refrigerator to reveal a row of Diet Pepsis. The gesture was kind, but I wasn't looking at the sodas, instead distracted by the exhaustion in his eyes. The sheriff was definitely working overtime after he'd had to fire his last partner. The fact that she was also someone he'd once dated didn't help matters. I couldn't imagine the emotional turmoil on top of his workload.

"Thanks, I've already had breakfast." I scooped Squeaks from my pocket and stooped to let him down on the floor. The mouse skittered across the gray carpet and sat at Sett's feet, chirping again. "I hate to ask but..." I pointed at the demanding little rascal.

"He wants coffee, right?" Sett huffed and straightened. He grabbed the coffee pot and poured a few drops into his palm and then crouched again, holding his hand for Squeaks to take a lick. As expected, Squeaks turned up his nose, whiskers twitching in the air.

I rolled my eyes. For a moment, the creepiness of the threat was forgotten. "He's too sophisticated to drink out of a hand."

Sett grumbled something unintelligible but did as Squeaks demanded, pouring more into a ceramic spoon rest in the shape of a rocket ship. My daughter had made it for him in art class and given it to him as an early Christmas present. Because he always rented science fiction movies from the shop, she knew he'd like the space theme.

"So what can I help you with, Noema?" Once he gave me his full attention, memory of the note flooded me.

I swallowed a lump and dug the paper out of my pocket. Unfolding it, I held it out to him. "This was taped to Mockbuster's door this morning. I'm sure it's nothing. Right?"

He didn't respond, only took the note and dropped his gaze. His slate eyes narrowed as they scanned the page. Concern creased his stony brow, and when he looked up at me, his throat bobbed with a hard swallow. "It's not nothing."

"Are you sure it's not a prank?" I hoped.

"Noema." He sucked in a breath and walked back to his desk. Instead of sitting, he hovered like the rain cloud. "It *could* be nothing, but you can—"

"'Never be too careful,'" I finished for him. "I know. Do you have a lead on who it might be and what they want?"

Sett sighed and beckoned for me to take a seat in one of the two chairs that faced his desk. "Not yet. The vandalism was unsettling." My movie-fan imagination got away from me. I pictured broken windows and eggs dripping down the side of the house. Maybe a flaming bag of doggie doo on the porch. Ick. "They marked his house with all kinds of Xs and angry faces."

"Odd." I still couldn't decide if spray paint was better or worse than my imagination. Once I sat perched on the edge of the chair, Sett finally took a seat too.

He swiped his palm over his face and sucked in a breath. "It could be targeting the house or the deputy for something worse. I took precautions and sent him to stay in Carmel." Carmel-by-the-sea was another quaint town nearby but not close enough for the deputy to commute back and forth. No wonder Sett was swamped with work. "I know the sheriff there, and he agreed to train my deputy for the time being."

"Judy got a note too, right?"

"Correct." He scooted the chair into the desk and rested his elbows on the desktop. His sharp stare leveled with me. "I instructed Judy to leave town while I sort this out." The hint of calm in his voice had dropped to a grinding growl. "She didn't listen."

Uh oh. He was going to insist I leave too. And I, also, didn't plan on listening.

"Noema—"

I held up my hand. "I can't."

"Can't what?"

"Leave town."

"Noema—"

"Has Judy's house been spray painted?" I asked, shifting the subject away from me. He shook his head. "And she's fine?"

"For now."

"It's Christmas, Sett."

"And as such, I wanted to suggest you extend your holiday trip until this is taken care of."

"We're not going. Mae and Wallace won't leave town with the threats ongoing, and I have half a dozen new traditions planned with them for the kids. It's their first holiday with people they can call their grandparents. If they're staying, I am too."

Silence hung heavy like fog blanketing the park. The air was thick, but I caught a slight scent of smoke from the sheriff's emotions. He was angry. Or frustrated. The two smelled the same. For an entire minute, the only sound came from Squeaks' lapping tongue as he slurped up the coffee.

When Sett spoke again, gentleness replaced the growl. "I just want you to be safe until I find this vandal. After all you've been through."

Two murders in two months. One of which pinned me between life and death and clearly left Sett shaken. But that was in the past and those criminals were locked away, and Sett wasn't my personal bodyguard.

"I can handle a little spray paint." Though I didn't love the idea of graffiti on Mockbuster. I stood, grabbed the note from his desk, and walked over to the kitchen, scooping Squeaks into my hand. Swiveling, I met Sett's gaze. "If you learn anything new, will you tell me?" When he didn't respond right away, words spilled out of me to avoid another stretch of silence. "Mae and I have all these cookie baking plans, and tree decorating. We're even going to try caroling. I can't imagine leaving their new family during Christmas."

"I can't promise I'll have information any time soon. With Mayor Fitz's ongoing campaign, he's not helping around here anymore. Plus, I have to work as security for the candidates' speeches and debates whenever I can."

"But you'll tell me?"

The muscles in his jaw rippled as he clenched his teeth. Seconds passed, and then he blew out a slow breath. "Of course I'll tell you."

The scent of vanilla coated the surrounding air as strongly as if I'd stepped inside a candy shop. I loved that Sett understood why I couldn't give up time with Grandmae—with our new family. The smell of love followed me as I thanked him and slipped out the door, leaving him to his paperwork and coffee.

CHAPTER 3
MIST-CONCEPTION

OUTSIDE, I tried to focus on the beauty in Bewitcher's Beach. Every cheerful detail. The bright red bows tied around black iron lamp posts. The big bells and holly that hung on the shop's door knobs. The display of Christmas sweaters in the boutique fashion store.

But the greens and reds and golds morphed into giant spray painted Xs in my mind's eye. I shook the image away. Everything was fine. Nothing had happened to Judy's house and she'd also received a threat.

"Everything is fine," I whispered to myself. The foggy morning kept everyone inside later than usual, leaving the cobblestone streets empty except for me.

And someone else.

Thump, thump, thump.

Footsteps thudded closer, and my heart matched the pounding. My imagination ran wild again. I tossed a glance over my shoulder but struggled to make out the figure in the fog. Why were they approaching so fast? Maybe whoever wrote the note had been watching me since I left Mockbuster. Adrenaline buzzed through my veins.

Without my permission, the overprotective side of me came out—wolfed out. As my fingernails extended into claws and my teeth sharpened to fangs, I whirled around and swiped a warning slash through the air.

The person was closer than I'd estimated, and my sharp claws sliced right through their black t-shirt. They doubled back, nearly stumbling over the uneven sidewalk. Crow's midnight eyes met mine as his brows shot up, disappearing behind the messy curls that hung over his forehead.

A gasp escaped me. I slapped a hand over my mouth as claws receded and my fangs mellowed. "I'm so sorry! You came up so fast. I was alone and spooked. Shoot, I'm sorry." My gaze raked over the mess I'd made of his inky outfit. "I've slashed your clothes to ribbons, I—do you wear anything other than black?" I glanced down at my own aquamarine sneakers, yellow spandex pants, and cerulean bodysuit beneath my Roller Shakes hoodie, suddenly realizing how kind it was for Crow to agree to attend this class with me. The rebellious reaper who lived for horror movies, whiskey, and boxing was certainly not the stereotypical attendee for a Friday morning step-aerobics class full of soccer moms.

He'd definitely done this for me.

Stretched skin over the scythe-shaped scar twitched as he smirked. He pinched the hem of his shirt with two fingers and tilted his head side-to-side. "Black brings out my eyes," he joked, fluttering his eyelashes. "Also, this shredded look is pretty fly."

A laugh bubbled out of me. "Pretty fly? Have you been spending too much time with the young crowd at Roller Shakes?"

"Way too much time," he said, eyes wide and feigning as though he was disturbed. "I hope those witches hurry up recreating the protection spell. You wouldn't believe the fights that break out there."

"Fights? At the roller rink?"

"Yeah, a skater shoves another skater, and suddenly I'm in between two middle-schoolers swinging punches." He tapped a dark spot just above his scar. "See this bruise? Noodle socked me right in the cheekbone with a tentacle." The little shapeshifter boy had never been known to lash out like that before. But lately children teased him for being stuck in the form of an octopus.

"Does that happen a lot?" I sucked in a rush of air as a humble epiphany dawned on me. "Don't tell me Halen and Dio do that too." The rowdier two of my pups had been known to rough house on more than one occasion. Even if the mysterious perpetrator had never stripped Bewitcher's Beach of the woven spell that warded us from fights, attacks, and crimes, their wrestling wouldn't be stopped. As I understood it, people must intend harm on one another before the protection spell would literally whirl them away like a subtle breeze. I looked up at the sky, but the low clouds blocked my view. Though we could never see the protection spell, most imagined it like a giant blanket wrapped around the town, keeping us all safe and warm.

He shrugged sheepishly. "They've been known to scuffle."

"Oh no...They'll get an earful when they get home from school today."

Crow waved the suggestion away. "Nah, I'm not worried about the kids. It's the parents that I have to keep my eye on. With this protection spell gone, I think people are just on edge."

"That on top of two killers who struck in less than two holidays." A low growl rumbled in my chest, warding away the heebie jeebies before I nearly wolfed out again. I pulled out the note and showed him the threat that triggered my claws and fangs earlier. A curl fell over his forehead but didn't mask the concern wrinkling his brow. I shared the new plan to stay in town for Christmas with Mae and Wallace.

When I finished, he reached for my hand and gave it a quick squeeze. "How are you doing? Worried? I know how it feels to be...threatened." Crow had come to Bewitcher's Beach seeking refuge from a stalker who'd tracked him here. Thankfully, the disturbed intruder had been arrested and locked away after killing a college student and then attempting to kill both me and Crow.

"I'm a little on edge. But it's Christmas, so I refuse to let this vandal ruin it for the kids." After Halloween and November celebrations were tainted by spooky murders, all the pressure fell on Christmas to dazzle and make dreams come true.

His dark eyes twinkled. "Speaking of Christmas, I wanted to ask you something."

Would he ask us to be official? My heart flipped. We'd been dating, casual dates, for a couple of weeks now. Nothing more than hand-holding and a peck on the cheek. Was I ready for more?

"I know we're calling this step aerobics class a date. And the movie nights are fun." He raked his fingers through his hair. "But I want to take you on a real date." I grinned. All thoughts of threats were ancient history now. "I'd planned to do it after your trip, but now we can have a holiday date. What do you think?"

We stopped in front of Aerobics Alive. I'd barely noticed the fog had burned off and the people that were milling about, opening their shops, walking their dogs, arriving to class. Even the sun came out, though the winter chill ran deep. Shining rays couldn't warm us through the icy breeze. His eyes shined as he awaited my answer. I brushed past him, grabbing the studio's door handle.

With a smirk on my face, I shot him a glance over my shoulder and yanked the door open. "Count me in."

I slipped inside, Crow at my heels. Wooden floorboards creaked beneath my sneakers, and gossip fizzed through the room full of women. Half-ponytails swished back and forth as they chattered and laughed, hands on hips. Holiday stickers decorated the front window, and a line of lush green garland was tacked to the windowsill in loops. A tall Christmas tree glittered with twinkling lights in the corner by the restroom. The studio was awash with colors, both neon, since Miss Raven had decorated the place in the 80s, and newly added reds and greens. I waved to Celeste, a mom I knew from the kids' soccer team, and Mae. Even Bette was here, possibly to get away from the argument with her mom. As a ghost, Hattie never saw the point in exercising, but Bette enjoyed the social aspect and booming music.

I squeezed past elbows and wiggled my way to the far wall lined with equipment.

The squat, bald mayor stood in front of me in basketball shorts and a lime green tank top. Fitz paused and blinked at me before smiling. The poor guy looked about as out of place as Crow, but at least the mayor had the sense not to dress like a black hole. He handed me a flier from the stack in his hand. *Vote Fitz Feet for safe streets!* Below the bold lettering were the dates and details of his upcoming speech.

Crow nodded toward the front of the room. "Campaigning during class? Don't let Miss Raven find out."

The mayor's grin only broadened. "I've got to stay sharp with the competition. Dr. Pitt gave me the idea."

"Your opponent gave you campaigning ideas?" I asked.

"Of course." His voice was as cheerful as ever. If anybody

could *sound* like a big red bow, it was Mayor Fitz. "I encouraged him to run. He'll replace me when I'm governor or senator." He glanced over his shoulder and then leaned closer. "But he can't win just yet."

Miss Raven, the retired reaper and workout instructor, shouted at everyone to get their equipment. Celeste skipped ahead of me to grab a step platform, and a flood of soccer moms shuffled into place. Mayor Fitz disappeared between leggy women twice his height. He reminded me a bit of Ferris Bueller in *Ferris Bueller's Day Off* with his spirited approach to everything. Though unlike the movie, Fitz didn't cause trouble. If only I could create a character as charming as Bueller for my screenplay...

Buzzing activity snapped me from the daydream. People in bright colors swirled around me, chatting, stretching, or jogging in place. I tore my gaze from the sea of spandex before it sent me into a dizzy spell. I could only hope I wouldn't trip over my own two feet in front of everyone. Squeezing past elbows, I ducked across the room to grab a small pair of dumbbells and a step platform.

I hurried to set up my equipment between Crow and Mae by the window. Bette took the spot by the window in front of us, and I realized why she'd joined class. Outside, a tattooed boy with a mohawk waited by the glass. I snorted at the memory of Hattie calling his hairstyle dinosaur spikes. His tattoos were barely visible, cracked and faint on ashy skin, and it seemed he wore a backpack beneath his shirt. A bulge under the fabric gave him a hunched look that clearly didn't deter Bette. The teenage ghost gave him a little wave before Miss Raven barked at her to pay attention.

The instructor clapped louder until Bette focused on her and everyone quieted. Behind Miss Raven, a neon backlit sign read Aerobics Alive. Painted on the wall beneath was her slogan "A workout a day will keep the reaper away!" A large black boombox blasted the upbeat tune of Aqua's "Barbie Girl". If this scene were a movie, we'd be adjusting our legwarmers in a *Flashdance* ballet studio.

"Chest up," the instructor called as she flicked her fluffy bangs from her face. "Breathing it out. Let's take it up, up, down, down in five, six, seven, eight."

Everyone stepped up with both feet on their small platforms and then returned to the floor. I scanned the crowd of women and suppressed a giggle when my eyes landed back on Crow. His ripped shirt billowed as he hopped up onto the platform. The dark clothes stuck out like a bruised thumb. When he noticed me looking, he gave me a sideways grin and mouthed Miss Raven's count. He waved for me to keep up though he'd also fallen a beat behind. *Five, six, seven, eight!*

On the next count, Mae marched to the side instead of up as the instructor announced. The half-dragon's face shimmered under the bright studio lights, and the light sweat accentuated the hint of scales beneath her skin.

"Did you hear?" Her red eyes flashed with the promise of gossip. "The coroner received one of those threatening notes too."

"What?" My stomach dropped as my feet stepped up.

A frown cracked her ashy plum lipstick. "Mhm. I just heard about it from Celeste. She lives two doors down from the coroner. This is getting out of control. It scared the poor man so badly he decided to take his holiday out of town. He packed up and went to Tahoe for Christmas."

"By himself?" The thought tugged at my heartstrings.

"Oh no. He has family in Tahoe," she said between huffs.

A jolt of relief boosted my energy. Everybody should be with family for the holidays. I wiped my brow and scrambled to stay on count. My lungs burned each time I stepped up. When my legs wobbled, I prayed I wouldn't miss the step and face-plant right through Bette's ghostly shape.

The workout was picking up now, demanding we swing our arms as we hop one foot on the platform. Mae stopped the swoop of one arm to adjust the red sweat band around her fore-head, and I took it as an excuse to stop too. Just to gulp a few breaths.

"Water!" Miss Raven screeched. *Thank heavens.* Everyone else stopped and swiped their water bottles. I nearly collapsed as I crouched to snatch my drink off the ground. Guzzling, I gasped for breaths in between every sip.

A sudden shift in smells sparked a tickle in my throat. I coughed, nearly choking on a drop of water. Smoke stung my nose. The heady char of anger. Eyeing the room, I expected to spot anger on someone's face. Everyone was sweaty and desperate for air, but nobody frowned.

Mae snapped the top back on her water bottle and sidled closer to me again. "In any case, I'm unsettled about all this commotion. I'd much prefer to go back to reporting a shortage of Christmas trees or Cliff's harassment. These notes give me the heebie jeebies." She quoted the slang my son Halen wanted to make popular. He'd carried his camcorder around town spooking people from bushes as he tried getting them to say the slang on camera. "My baby senses the stress and it gives her an awful rash."

I glanced over my shoulder to where her *baby* was curled in her husband's lap. Wallace sat on a bench leaning against the back wall with his eyes closed and the poodle nestled in the fluff of his robe. Smoke stung my nose and throat as I sucked in a breath.

At the sound of a scream, my head whipped around, eyes locked on the front of the room. I searched for a downed soccer mom who'd stepped wrong and slipped off her platform.

Maybe with nothing more than a bruised tailbone. But the screaming intensified along with the growing, choking scent of smoke. Copper and amber flames ate away at the baseboards behind Miss Raven. The fire released puffs of gray as it stretched, catching the curtains and garland along the large window above. Flames climbed up the Christmas tree. With its hold on the branches, the fire spread at the speed of light, eating away at the pine needles and the lights' plastic wires. The floorboards burned the fastest, igniting the studio's ground like fuel in a bonfire. It started low but licked up the tree quicker than my brain could make sense of the situation.

After a moment of shock, chaos erupted.

Colorful spandex-clad bodies leaped off their platforms and trampled the equipment in a mad dash for the door. Gray and black smoke filled the small studio as I remained frozen, unable to react. Both me and the old wood-framed building were at the mercy of the flames.

Crow grabbed my wrist and pulled me toward the door. The poodle yipped and yapped, furiously scrambling to get out of Wallace's arms. Mae woke her husband, who hadn't been alerted by the dozens of shrieks. The four of us filed out the door with thick heat at our backs.

Erratic pulse thudded in my ears as we hurried away from the studio and spun around to see the damage.

Flames swallowed the northern side of Aerobics Alive. Heat radiated in waves that gradually pushed us back further and further as we stared up at the destruction. A sharp pain sliced across my chest. I'd blame it on the intensity of the workout if I didn't know myself better.

It hurt to see someone's livelihood, their job—their *home*—destroyed right before our very eyes. Like me, Miss Raven lived in a loft above the studio.

Wailing fire trucks echoed through town. Miss Raven's

voice lifted above the other noise as she continued the class right there in the middle of the street. "At least we got a great workout in, right ladies?" She was nothing if not positive, but a quiver in her voice betrayed her demeanor.

And I couldn't blame her. If Mockbuster burned...if I were her, I'd be in shambles. I swallowed hard, my throat squeezing from the smoke and emotion and...another withering stench filled the air. Ammonia. The smell of fear surrounded us. Especially me.

Despite the chaos of colors and fire and early morning exhaustion, my mind was clear. Clear enough to think of the threat. We'd abandoned the premises, but Aerobics Alive wasn't spared.

This better not give the vandal any ideas.

CHAPTER 4
AEROBICS ABLAZE

THE FIRE DEVOURED the studio's northern wall about as fast as Squeaks and I finished a bag of popcorn. Watching the wood turn to kindling turned my stomach and sank my heart for Miss Raven. She spent the majority of her life inside that building.

I looped my arm around her, offering a bit of comfort. I knew the worry of losing a business all too well. Though I'd solved the murder just in time to bring customers back into Mockbuster and before I lost the building over unpaid rent.

Scattered coughs rippled through the gathered onlookers. Everyone cleared their throats, covering their mouths and noses with the fabric of their shirts or their hands. One-by-one, they approached to give the instructor their condolences.

Crow patted Miss Raven's back and then bid me goodbye with a kiss on the cheek. Roller Shakes wasn't going to run itself, but I hated to see him go. I wouldn't mind his shoulder to lean on after the unsettling morning. As he abandoned the crowd, I focused on Mae and Miss Raven.

The half-dragon nearly squeezed the life out of her little poodle. "Of course I won't charge you rent while the studio is shut down," she said. "We'll get this figured out." Babette barked in support, and when Mae tugged Miss Raven in for a hug, they squished the pup into a poodle sandwich. Since Mae owned some of the buildings in Bewitcher's Beach and rented them out, she had a vested interest in the studio's return to business. Not to mention her fierce respect and love for Miss Raven. Both women lifted their chins, resilient in the face of a disaster, but I caught the stricken looks. Fine lines tugged along Mae's frown and Miss Raven's pinched brow. The earthy scent of sadness swirled around them as though a cloud descended over their heads and unleashed a torrent of rain. They leaned on one another.

"Insurance should cover the cost of rebuilding, but I know they'll drag their feet with payout," Mae said, brows knitted. "They always take so darned long to investigate before they give any money. Speaking of investigations." She tilted her head to me, eyes sharp. "Will you be sniffing out if this was intentional? Finding someone who smells like a sailor perhaps?" The reference to the fishy smell of guilt had my pulse thudding erratically. Why would Mae immediately assume foul play?

The notes...She knew plenty about the threats since she was writing a column about them.

"Were you threatened, Miss Raven?" I asked. I didn't want to believe the worst because the worst meant Mockbuster might be next.

Wetness shined in her dark eyes, but she blinked it away as she sucked in a sharp breath. Mae was already nodding. "You don't have to be Miss Positivity for us, Raven. Let it out."

She didn't let it out. Miss Raven brushed at her fluffy black bangs and sniffed. The flush of emotion in her face washed away and she became her usual pale self again. "I was the first to get a note, but I ignored it. I thought it was just a mean-spirited prank. At worst, I expected graffiti like what happened to the deputy."

"A prank was my first suspicion too!" I jumped in. "Maybe the note and the fire are unrelated. Could this have been an accident? Maybe the boombox overheated? Or the heater malfunctioned?" A wave of hope swelled within me but was quickly dashed on the rocks.

Miss Raven shook her head. "The music was still playing when the fire started, and the building didn't have heating. Besides, it was already too hot in the studio from all the sweaty bodies."

I racked my brain for the source of most fires. "What about faulty wiring? Or did you have a candle melting?"

The instructor's jet-black ponytail swished back and forth as she denied both. "Even during yoga, I never melt candles because Celeste has asthma. But I know nothing about wiring. The building is rather old."

"Old, yes, but regularly inspected and updated," Mae said. She thrust a long fingernail in the air, and the sudden movement made the poodle in her arms yip and shiver with fear or excitement—thankfully, I couldn't smell animals' emotions too. Unless they were shifters in their creature forms.

"Could you have left the stove lit or the oven on upstairs?" I was clawing at straws now.

Again, she shook her head. "The fire came from the ground, not above."

She was right. The fire seemed more intentional by the second. My stomach churned, and I regretted the Diet Pepsi I'd pounded for an early-morning caffeine boost.

A building didn't go up in flames for no reason, but maybe it was as simple as a nearby string of Christmas lights burning too hot. Perhaps the tree was already drying up.

Half an hour passed until the fire department successfully

tamed the beast. All the while, we gaped, and a crowd collected both to console Miss Raven and out of pure curiosity.

Sett arrived, a low-marching stone of determination. After speaking with the fire marshal, he strode over to us. His giant wings folded close to his back as he offered Miss Raven's arm a reassuring squeeze.

The sheriff's deep voice was laced with concern as his eyes slid from the crumbled wall back to the aerobics instructor. "If you're feeling up to it, I have a few questions I'd like to ask to help assess the situation. I've spoken with the fire marshal, and she has reason to believe this incident was no accident."

"Is that for sure?" I blurted.

Sett frowned, and his wings flexed slightly, lifting and then returning to tight arches around his muscular shoulders. He ran his tongue along his top teeth beneath his lips. His voice dropped low as he kept the information securely within our circle. "I'm surprised you can't smell it, Noema."

I tilted my chin to the sky and sniffed. An array of emotions swirled through the dwindling crowd. The peppermint of curiosity was the strongest scent with ammonia from worry or fear as a close second. Buried beneath the emotions, the strange burn of benzene stung my nose.

"Gasoline," I whispered, trying to determine if the icky but sweet scent came from someone's anger or if it was real gasoline.

Sett's head dipped with a slight nod. "Correct. And from the marshal's preliminary check, the gas lines are still intact. No leaks."

"I told you!" Mae said. The poodle barked in support. "All my buildings are regularly inspected and updated. I keep my friends safe."

After Miss Raven confessed to having received—and ignored—a threat, Sett pulled out a notepad. He asked detailed questions and recorded her answers. *Did you notice anyone following you? No. Is there anyone who might want to cause you harm? No.*

The round of questions halted when the fire marshal called Sett, and he excused himself. He turned but not without a lingering look of warning shot in my direction. Though I couldn't smell his emotions, his thoughts were as clear as the pictures in the books he read to children at the library. The threats were on his mind as much as mine. Stony footsteps hit heavy against the cobblestone as he marched toward the ashy building with his hands tucked into the pockets of his navy police coat.

Despite the heat of rising emotions and the lingering warmth from the descending fire, an icy blast sent shivers down my arms. I ran my palms over my bare arms, suddenly freezing as an apparition appeared. The ghostly being seemed to come from nowhere.

Mae yelped as the figure manifested into the shape of Cliff Conflick, the man who had been murdered only months before. The wealthy plastic surgeon had purchased a beachfront home from Mae before he was poisoned, and his spirit became tethered to the town. None of us knew what tethered him here. Unlike Hattie, this ghost's manifestation was erratic, sometimes almost solid enough to be a living person. Other times scratchy and faded like a fuzzy television screen buzzing with static on a broken channel. Likely because he was rushing the process of learning how to solidify his ghostly body enough to interact with objects. According to Hattie, who'd been a ghost a long time, the process was gradual. But Cliff was as impatient in death as he'd been in life.

The tall, hunched man looked just as he had when he'd died, wearing an open button-down shirt, slacks that cut off just above the ankle, and loafers with no socks. His frosted hair lightened his spiky style with blonde tips.

"Good riddance!" Cliff huffed as he surveyed the damage. "It was a dump and needed to be replaced anyway." The apparition filled in solidly as if he was standing alive between us. He shot Mae a look. "Just like my beach house." Cliff jumped on every opportunity to complain. He was *too rich, too smart, and too cultured for the likes of us.*

"Then why did you buy it?" Mae asked.

He clucked his tongue. "Because my girlfriend liked the view."

Mae waved her hands through his manifestation, causing the apparition to blink and then vanish as if she'd clicked off a TV set. "Now is not the time to harass me, Mr. Conflick. I'm stressed enough." She sniffed and petted the curly fur on the crown of the poodle's head.

When his apparition materialized again, Cliff shot a daggered gaze at me. "You've been avoiding me." Of course I was. Who wanted to be told their love for their home was pathetic? "You look a little sickly right now. Get your head together and then we'll talk."

Before I could ask why, he disappeared. His ghostly shape came in and out of view like a teleporting body as he headed for the other side of town.

Did he want to corner me and mock me for living in a loft above my shop? Or ask why I'd chosen to settle in a "pathetic place such as this"? I wiped my palm over my face and shook off the thoughts. Like Mae said, now wasn't the time to worry about Cliff's judgment.

I had more important questions to consider. Like who wanted to destroy Aerobics Alive and why.

Bewitcher's Beach was still recovering from two murders. The note's threat resurfaced in my mind like a relentless villain in a B movie. Odors mixed. Both ammonia and smoke—my own fear and anger—permeated the surrounding air.

Sett returned. "As you know, our fire department is small." Small indeed. Only three firefighters were employed, and they mostly serviced the surrounding towns since fire in Bewitcher's Beach was as rare as a month without a festival or holiday. "Since I've worked in tandem with the fire marshal for other towns, I'll be working as the investigator on this case as well. For now, we're evaluating the safety of the structure so we can stay inside long enough to study the damage. It's in your best interest to pay Doctor Pitt a visit. Each of you should have your lungs examined after inhaling smoke." He faced me, eyes serious and the flat line of his mouth stern. "That means you too, Noema. I heard you were the last to exit the building."

"I'm fine—"

"I'll be sending everyone from that class for an examination. You're no different."

My heart hiccupped. *You're no different.* I was dating Crow, not Sett, so why did that comment feel like a punch to the gut? Because we were supposed to be friends? "Right," I finally said.

With that, he gave us both a curt nod and turned away. I was no different than Miss Raven, or Celeste, or Mayor Fitz, or Mae. Just another townsperson.

I swallowed a sigh. Though my lungs felt fine and full of the fresh, salty sea air, I headed for the clinic across town. With each long stride, my mind unclouded and I relished a minute alone to think. What would the fire investigation turn up? If the creep threatening everyone was involved, maybe this would expose them. Surely they left evidence, or maybe a witness saw them lurking outside the class.

A towering figure appeared in front of me. My heart shot to my throat. Cliff's scratchy apparition stood on the sidewalk only a step away. Only halfway to the clinic, I'd lost my moment of solace. Cliff crossed his arms and leered down at me. I could simply walk right through his wispy, ghostly frame, but my feet froze like wet skin on ice.

"Time to talk," he said. "You and everyone else who botched my murder investigation trapped me here."

"Botched? I was the one who got your killer put behind bars, and I definitely didn't trap you anywhere." I mirrored his power stance with folded arms and a lifted chin. As a werewolf, I stood taller than most women, and though I didn't match Cliff's height—especially since he floated a few inches above the ground—I wasn't dwarfed by him either.

"Yeah, botched, ruined, mishandled. Whatever you want to call it, my case took way too long to solve. I've done my research since becoming *this* monstrosity." He swiped a hand through his midsection, temporarily making half his body disappear like a cloud of smoke. The shape materialized again. "When investigations are resolved in a timely manner, it helps release the person's spirit within days. But of course *I* had to die in this backwoods embarrassment of a town where everything takes a decade to get done. Now, my spirit is tied to some junk here and I don't know what it is. If I find out, then I can carry it with me like your flapper girl friend does with that hideous jewel. Or I can have you torch it for all I care."

Torch it? I couldn't help but think of the flames devouring the Christmas tree in Aerobics Alive. Was that just a poor choice of words? Or had Cliff's harassment devolved into vandalism and arson?

He continued, unaware of my theorizing. "I just want to get out of this pathetic place whether it's movement or passing on, and since I've heard you're quite the investigator, you'll help me break free."

"But—"

"Or else I'll haunt you for the rest of your life."

"Why me?" I challenged, refusing to back down from the intimidating apparition. He owed me his gratitude, not his demands. A devilish grin spread across his face and made me want to sock him right in the throat. If I tried, my fist would simply pass right through him.

"Because, in my research, I've learned that any objects used in the investigation or at the crime scene itself can tether the spirit. The last object I touched was a stupid VHS tape."

Curses. From what Hattie had told me about her own death and her tether to the costume jewelry, he was right. "So let me get this straight. You want me to give you the tape so you can carry it with you and leave Bewitcher's Beach?" If I recalled correctly, Cliff died holding a tape of *The Swan Princess.*

"Is that what it was? I'm not carrying that junk around." He leaned down, meeting me nose-to-nose. "Just burn it. Burn all the tapes I rented."

"I'm not burning my shop's stock."

"Then prepare to hear me sing Rick Astley's 'Never Gonna Give You Up' every night when you're trying to sleep. *Forever.*" He fiddled with something in his hand. "Unless you want me to try to destroy the tape myself, but my ability to hold and touch things is shoddy and dangerous. For you, anyway. I'm already dead. It's your call."

Before I could bark back, he flickered away, scratchy and buzzing in an unstable manifestation. He must have heard I was strictly a rock-and-roll fan—all Van Halen, Ronnie James Dio, Stevie Nicks, and Bon Jovi for me. I wouldn't survive one night of listening to pop.

Great. Another threat to haunt me all through Christmas. Not to mention I now had Rick Astley's lyrics stuck in my head.

CHAPTER 5
RISE FROM THE ASHES

AROUND FOUR THE NEXT MORNING, I woke up in a sweat, claws out and ears listening for the crackle of a fire. The kids were safely having a sleepover at Everland Theater with Bette, but I'd wanted my own bed. All at the cost of a good night's rest.

The glowing red numbers on my clock mocked me. 4:49. Only two hours until I had to wake up and get ready for the day. I groaned and yanked the quilt over my head.

"Too early," I muttered. Pillowy softness lulled me into a restless doze. Echoes of Rick Astley's song and Cliff's demand had me raising my hackles.

But those were nothing compared to the note.

At least Cliff didn't threaten anything that'd upset my family like the note had. Though the kids wouldn't love listening to him sing, the disturbance paled in comparison to the danger directed at our home. Unless the note, the fire, and Cliff's demand that I burn the VHS tape were related.

I couldn't let late-night theories twist my mind. I threw myself to the other side of the bed, stuffing my fist under the flat pillow.

The only comfort that allowed my muscles to melt into the mattress was the plan to help clean Aerobics Alive. Sett assured me that the fire marshal was finished taking pictures and gathering information for the arson investigation, so we'd been cleared to enter the partial building. Dozens of Miss Raven's students coordinated the event to clear out the ash and debris.

By restoring the damage, maybe the vandal would get the message that they couldn't scare us away. Their crime couldn't control us.

Finally, my eyelids grew heavy and I drifted to sleep again —until my alarm blared...

"Good morning Bewitcher's Beach!" the radiocaster bellowed. I blinked and released a huff, already dreading having agreed to do an aerobics class this morning. Of course I wanted to support Miss Raven, but the thought of exercising this early on a weekend almost made me wolf out. At least the class was next door. The Oyster Inn offered Miss Raven the meeting hall for a small fee until Aerobics Alive was up and running again. "It's a chilly Saturday but no rain in sight," the radiocaster chattered away. "According to resident reporter, Mae Wildefyre, rain would have been a welcome blessing yesterday. But thanks to the good-natured citizens of Bewitcher's Beach, Aerobics Alive will, in fact, be alive again soon. Now the question is, will the weather cooperate for Mayor Fitz's upcoming campaign rally?"

I slapped the off button and rolled out of bed.

Saturday morning cartoons blared from the box television in the living room. The kids had returned to the loft for breakfast since our ghostly neighbors didn't eat and therefore did not store food.

I yawned as I dragged myself to the threshold between the kitchen and living room. A night of tossing and my stomach churning left me dragging. Four lazy pups flopped on the sofa or the floor or laid flat on their stomach across the coffee table. They munched cream cheese and strawberry flavored Toaster Strudels.

I downed a Diet Pepsi and a brown sugar Pop Tart. The load of sugar should get me through a morning of exercise and an afternoon of cleaning. If I didn't crash first.

"Let's get moving, my class starts in five minutes!" I shouted from the kitchen where I gulped the last bit of bubbles from my drink and snagged a leftover cracker from an abandoned Lunchables package.

While they pulled on their sneakers, I fitted my turquoise visor. The visor's band kept my curls out of my face while my wolf ears held the hat securely in place.

The five of us hopped down the spiral staircase that led from the loft and into Mockbuster. The video rental shop was stocked full of candy, popcorn, and hundreds of VHS tapes, including the newest blockbuster releases like *Jerry Maguire, Jurassic Park,* and *Liar Liar.* I'd yet to decorate, though. The stupid note and scary fire had derailed my day. I hated how dark and drab the shop looked compared to the rest of town.

"Later," I promised, whispering to Squeaks. He perched on a miniature doll's bed Stevie had nestled between the keyboard and the computer monitor at the register desk. During winter, the mouse preferred to stay in as much as possible, sleeping his life away like a hibernating bear. He came downstairs so he could watch the goings on in Bewitcher's Beach from the big windows. When he wasn't snoozing.

Two doors down, The Oyster Inn was teeming with life. Half of Aerobics Alive may have become ash, but the energy of its slogan was stronger than ever. We were alive, well, and ready to bounce it out at the meeting hall.

The inn's holiday decorations captured the feel of a mall during Christmas. Garlands adorned every door frame and hung from the ceiling. Massive red bows were tied to the corners of the front desk and the bartop in the lobby. Twinkling white lights reflected in the shiny marble floor and matched the glistening chandeliers. All of the meeting hall tables and chairs had been stacked against the walls to open the space. A Christmas tree with fake snow stood in the far corner of a stage often used for town meetings. The snow was as bright as everyone's shiny white sneakers.

Class attendees exchanged gossip while they stretched and waited for Miss Raven to finish setting up. She perched a borrowed boombox on a chair near the tree and cranked the volume to full blast. Whitney Houston's "I Wanna Dance With Somebody" blared, loud enough to wake the forest animals. While kids danced around on the stage, their moms lined up in front of Miss Raven in organized rows and copied her movements.

"Reach! Reach!" Miss Raven belted the instructions to raise our hands high above our heads. "Imagine you're pulling a branch from a tree and cracking it over your knee. Lift those legs!"

A dark figure in the lobby caught the corner of my eye, and goosebumps rippled down the back of my neck. Who was watching me? I twisted in between sets of "branch breaking" to see Crow arrive with a new black shirt, identical to the one from the day before but without the slashes from my claws. He lifted his chin in a curt nod as he jogged into the room and joined me at the back of class.

Without the step platforms, we followed a basic aerobics routine of jumping jacks, high knees, and my least favorite, hopping lunges. Each time I jumped and tried to switch which leg was in front, I toppled to the side like the leaning tower of Noema. Crow caught me before I fell into a sweaty heap on the ground.

"I balance better on four paws," I felt the need to explain myself.

"So are you disappointed about the road trip?" Crow asked after returning me upright. I blinked at him. In all the excitement—and with all the threats—I'd emotionally shelved the anticipation. As much as I wanted to understand the magical book I'd found and if I was related to the author, I wanted my home and shop safe first. Mostly, I wanted Christmas to be magical and family-focused for my kids. And I supposed it wasn't so bad that the kids *didn't* miss out on the last week of school. Class activities promised snowman crafts and gift exchanges. His arms swooped over his head in a jumping jack, drawing my attention. "I know you were excited to visit Senna and learn about *The Book of Prophecies*."

I frowned. "I *was* excited. But I won't celebrate another Christmas alone, or abandon Mockbuster with a threat looming."

Crow's lips twisted, dragging the hook's tip of his facial scar down. "If you can convince Mae and Wallace to go, everyone will keep an eye on the shop for you. Sett would never let anything happen to your home. Doesn't he call himself your backup?"

Hearing the nickname Sett and I had given one another coming from Crow's mouth only soured my stomach. The spicy, sweet scent of pineapple pizza exuded from my sweat. I sneezed at the smell of confusion and offered a shrug in response. "Not really. He's just everybody's backup because he protects the whole town."

Crow stayed silent, but the odor that came from him said more than enough. It had been a long time since I smelled steamed broccoli, considering I never forced the yucky vegetable on myself or my children. The icky sulfur was the culprit of one particular emotion I hadn't recognized in anyone since Dio outscored Halen on a math test. *Jealousy.*

"Well," he spoke up after a few minutes, "I'll watch Mockbuster if you'd like, and when I can't be there, I know Hattie will take over."

"That was the plan," I said. "Bette was supposed to work at Mockbuster while I was gone, but I know I can't change Mae's mind. Thanks anyway. It's tempting. I'm dying to find out if this mark really is part of the prophecy." I touched a small tattoo in the shape of wings or wolf ears or—I wasn't sure what had appeared on the skin of my collarbone. A young witch I'd met believed it foretold that I was the chosen witch from *The Book of Prophecies.* If she was right, the book might lead me to the family I'd lost when I became a werewolf at nineteen years old.

The exercise fired up my muscles and sent my temperature skyrocketing. Once cool-down started, conversations cropped up. Mae chatted with Celeste, loudly complaining about Cliff's appearance at the fire yesterday. "And would you believe he even showed up at my house? The man actually harassed me at my own home. He called the house I'd sold him a 'beachfront dump'! I shouldn't have bought it back after he died because now I'm stuck. If I sell it, he'll just haunt whoever buys it. And that will be on my conscience forever. I'd never do that to a homeowner."

Who else had Cliff harassed? Miss Raven once said he'd blamed her for failing as a reaper. Would that really push him to set fire to Aerobics Alive? Did he think he was tethered to something there and when torching the studio didn't work, he demanded I destroy the VHS tape?

Celeste shook her head and took a swig from a water bottle. "If Cliff ever stops haunting the beach house, I'd put an offer on it. I've always wanted a view of the shore." She palmed her chest and let out a little gasp. "And that wraparound porch. I'd just die."

Mae spluttered, smoke emitting from her nostrils as was occasional for half-dragons. "I daresay that comment was in poor taste, Celeste. Cliff died right after he bought it."

As soon as the stretching ended, Crow snaked his arm around my waist and planted a kiss on my cheek. The reaper's touch was chilly but not cold enough to give my scorching wolf fever relief. With our bodies so close, I only burned hotter and wanted to slip away from the stickiness of our shared sweat.

"I'll make sure the pups eat lunch and take water breaks," Crow said. The kids planned to roller skate all day while I volunteered. It was the best alternative I had to avoid disappointment. Before Aerobics Alive was attacked, the five of us planned to decorate Mae and Wallace's house for the holidays. Cleaning up the destruction postponed those plans, and their little hearts were crushed.

I shot Crow two thumbs up and followed the trail of women outside and across town. We gathered in front of Aerobics Alive, chatting with one another as we awaited permission to cross the yellow tape. Other townspeople joined in. Humans, pixies, shapeshifters, and half-dragons alike all offered their services to help Miss Raven rebuild. Triton, gangly human and owner of next door's sweet shop, chatted with Mayor Fitz, who was boasting about his reelection campaign.

"As you can see," Fitz said, opening his arms like his presence here was on display, "a vote for me is a vote for helping. I'm involved in the community." He was laying it on thick, knowing Dr. Pitt was a beloved man in Bewitcher's Beach. Though the gentle, soft-spoken doctor was one of Fitz's closest buddies, it was clear the mayor wasn't ready to give up his role just yet. Even to a friend.

Mae, Celeste, and Chanel joined the humans. Their conversation shifted to gossip about a builder who remodeled several homes in town. Even Wallace was here. He'd shed his bathrobe and donned a frayed pair of jeans and an old *Bewitcher's Beach Fifth Annual Fall Festival* T-shirt. The only people missing from the crowd were the vampires who dwelled in Bewitcher's Beach. Scattered clouds didn't offer enough defense from the sun's unpredictable appearances.

Once Sett gave Miss Raven the "okay," we ducked under the caution barrier. I stopped next to the sheriff, feeling the cool air that hovered around his stony skin. "Are you positive this won't interfere with the investigation?"

Sett tilted his head and eyed me, rubbing his jaw. "We've already determined the point of origin, tagged anything that appeared to be evidence, and taken photos. The existing structures are solid and safe to be inside, but if you come across anything suspicious, I trust you'll let me know."

"Of course." I crossed my heart with one finger. "I'm here to help any way I can."

"You always are." His tone was harsh, but the softness in his slate eyes said otherwise. I caught the slight lift at the corner of his mouth before his expression returned to sternness. "Have you considered going on the trip to Shadowvale? I know you're worried about Mockbuster." He raised his hand to the charred wall in front of us. "But your safety comes first."

"I'm not planning on it, not unless Mae and Wallace can go with us. But they're more resolved than ever to stay and watch their rentals. She's setting up security cameras to catch the vandal on tape." Cliff's frosted tips and mean mug came to mind. I easily pictured him lurking and sneaking until a camera caught him in the act. "Did you know Cliff is pissed off at everyone who worked on his case? He blames us for trapping his spirit here."

"I've heard rumors," he said. He folded his arms, the thick muscles tightening against the sleeves on his forearms and around his biceps.

"Do you think he was targeting us while we were all at the class? At least to send a message? Mayor Fitz, Miss Raven, and I were all there, and we each played a role in his case." I wasn't part of Sett's investigation. This time. Still, I couldn't help but bounce ideas off of him. He was slow enough to think through each suggestion while I sped ahead and considered a case's every angle.

Sett's wings lifted in a shrug, and he released a low hum. "Interesting theory. I can add him to the list of suspects."

"List?" Curiosity would kill the wolf if I didn't stop prying. But the more I knew, the better I could protect myself.

Sett arched his eyebrow. "Yes, a list. Nothing solid, but I have to start with anyone who was seen near the building at the time of the fire. Basic things."

Before he could offer more information, if he was even willing to, Miss Raven raised her voice. "Today we're packing out everything that can be salvaged. Judy has kindly offered to use her expertise with repair spells on any damaged equipment." Like everyone else, my attention panned to the red-headed librarian at the back of the crowd. Her skin shimmered from her partial dragon ancestry, and her grin glowed with pride over her newfound skill with minor intention spells. Miss Raven pointed to a line of giant plastic recycling bins tucked just inside the caution tape's barrier. "If it looks like we can save an item with mild magic or basic repair, please load it into one of the blue bins."

Nods rippled through the group of volunteers before everyone set to work, picking through ashes. We dug out dumbbells from beneath rubble. I started at the northern wall where the neon sign had once hung and searched for the boombox, hoping it was intact for Miss Raven's sake. She'd used the same boombox since she'd opened Aerobics Alive and I couldn't picture her without it.

Christmas ornaments crushed beneath my sneakers. Red and gold bulbs popped as I picked through the mess and swept Christmas tree ashes and glass into a bin. Heat stung behind my eyes at the sight of the destroyed decorations.

After twenty minutes of moving pieces of the roof to dig out the boombox, I sighed and shot Miss Raven an apologetic glance though her back was to me. Everyone was busy working, and to my pleasant surprise, the plastic bins filled up fast. Since the fire had started in the far corner away from where the racks of dumbbells and step platforms were stored, most of the items were salvageable.

I retrieved my water bottle and took a swig as I walked to my next cleanup destination. Carefully stepping around the still-standing southwestern wall, I balanced my water bottle on a pile of rubble. Between the southern wall and the bathroom was a small closet where Miss Raven had stored her CD collection. If I couldn't salvage her boombox, maybe I'd dig out her CDs.

Twenty more minutes of searching yielded a magenta binder that had been dirtied with ash and soot. *I found it!* The aroma of my own excitement swirled around me, and the delicious scent of banana cream pie left me salivating. I hopped to my feet, CD collection in hand, and picked my way around the wall again.

Miss Raven's dark eyes sparkled as she accepted the binder. "I'm so glad my pop collection survived! Thank you." She patted my arm in gratitude and hugged the binder to her chest. "Any chance you came across the hip hop binder?"

"I'll keep looking," I said, "Maybe the entire collection can be saved." I hurried back to where the closet had been to find a piece of paper fluttering in the wind beneath my water bottle. As it flapped, I caught sight of a word: *warning*. Familiar slanted handwriting sent my blood whooshing in my ears. I reached for the note, but the breeze swept it away as soon as I lifted the weight of the bottle. Wind carried it out of my reach. On instinct, I dropped to all fours, shifting into my werewolf form where I could run faster and jump higher. My clothes fell in flutters around me, and I abandoned them, chasing after the paper. I leaped into the air, snatching the escaped note in my jaws. When my paws hit the ground, I pawed the paper from my sticky mouth and pinned it to the cobblestone behind Aerobics Alive.

If you've received an invitation to leave, consider this your final warning and tell the others. Move away before Christmas and never come back.

Fur raised between my haunches, and a low growl escaped my chest. The scent of smoky anger and ammonia's fear drifted from me. I lifted my head, turning from the view of the beach and back to the building. Someone inside Aerobics Alive left this note. A second note.

I snatched it again and padded around the wall to see through the wreckage to the dozens of bodies crouching, lifting, cleaning, talking, carrying rubble. It was a man in business casual I expected to spot. A man whose apparition flickered in and out of existence. But Cliff was nowhere to be seen, and I never felt the icy chill of his presence while cleaning.

If not an angry ghost, then who? None of these people would want to hurt Miss Raven or drive her away from Bewitcher's Beach. Not to mention me, or Judy, or the deputy. We'd all received the same first note... Would we get more? These were friends. People we considered family.

Despite my thick fur and the unusually warm sun for early December, I shivered.

CHAPTER 6
WARMING UP

THE FIRST TWO hours of salvaging equipment from Aerobics Alive was a success that left volunteers glowing with pride and sweat and hope for the reconstruction of one of Bewitcher's Beach's oldest buildings. Except for me. If I glowed, it was with nervous energy.

Behind the privacy of shrubbery, I shifted back to my human form and slipped into my clothes. I kept the note folded and inside my spandex bra where it only slightly chafed every time I swung my arm. There it'd stay safe and sound with no chance of slipping from a pocket. The note was evidence I intended to show Sett as soon as the cleanup crew dispersed.

Meanwhile, the paper poked into my armpit, serving as a good reminder to keep my eyes peeled for suspicious behavior. But after another hour of digging equipment out from dust and rubble, I didn't witness any unusual glances or overhear incriminating gossip. And when I sniffed out a hint of rotten fish, the guilt wasn't traceable to one single person. Like me, it was possible others felt a dash of shame that their businesses and livelihoods stood strong while Miss Raven suffered such a great loss. Smells were useless to me right now.

Maybe Sett's list would help me determine the culprit. The sheriff stayed to the bitter end to say goodbye to Miss Raven. Once we were the only two left lingering outside the studio, I tried to discreetly dig the note out of my bra.

"I found something," I said. My tongue stuck to the corner of my mouth as I focused on getting my fingers beneath the impossibly tight band. Sett tilted his head and then appropriately averted his gaze, pretending to take interest in a gull that perched on the top of a charred wall. The bird squawked and mimicked the angle of Sett's head. I tugged the note from where it was plastered between my moist skin and the bra that clung to me as if hanging on for life. *Shick!* The paper tore at the edge. I'd pulled it out but not without damaging it. "Curses!"

"I'd offer to help, but I have no idea what's going on." Sett's eyes dipped to my bra and I cringed, forcing an awkward smile. I was so focused on keeping the note safe I didn't consider how ridiculous I looked digging into my undergarments.

"It's a note," I said.

"And it was in your underwear?"

"Yes, in my underwear."

"Why?"

My blood boiled. "Because these stupid spandex outfits have no pockets!" The bra squeezed my torso, and I suddenly felt like a dog with a collar that fit too tightly. Sett only blinked at me, clueless. "You wouldn't understand, your coat alone has three pockets. Not to mention your pants." I waved wildly at his pockets until it dawned on me that I was pointing directly at his crotch. Heat rose to my cheeks. Embarrassment resembled the stink of fear. Ammonia rose around me but with the icky twang of body odor. Like when deodorant just didn't do the trick. I bit my lip before apologizing for the stink. Sett didn't need to be clued in on my embarrassment. I was the only one capable of smelling emotions. Thankfully.

Sett said nothing as he took the two parts of the note. When he pieced it together, he scanned the words until his slate eyes darkened to two storm clouds. "Out of the frying pan and into the fire," he muttered, repeating one of Mayor Fitz's cliches. "This vandal means business. Miss Raven didn't listen to the threat, so they attacked. And according to this"—he held up the note pinched between his thumb and forefinger—"they're going to strike again if she doesn't leave. I need to warn her. Also Judy, and—" His breath caught, and he eyed me. "Go on that road trip while I figure this out."

I bristled, my wolf ears folding back. So what if he wanted that? I wanted my kids to be with their Grandmae! I refused to run away and leave my home exposed to vandals—or an angry ghost. Not right now. Not right after I finally found the place I belonged and with the people I loved the most. "That's not happening."

"Noema—"

"That shop is my livelihood *and* my home. I won't lose it. Especially before Christmas. I'm not moving out of Bewitcher's Beach."

"What about the threat?"

"I don't let criminals control my life, nor do I trust them. Just because they claim they'll spare Mockbuster doesn't mean they actually will." I stood my ground. Sett grumbled something before he pursed his lips, jaw clenching. "But I'll send the kids to Grandmae's for a sleepover. They'll love it, and they'll be safe there. They've always had a great time sleeping over with Bette and Hattie."

Silence hung, stagnant and heavy like fog. The vandal couldn't tell me what to do any more than Sett. My gaze slid to the giant milkshake on wheels at the other side of town. Gratitude for Crow swelled within me. He never tried to tell me what to do.

After a momentary staredown, werewolf to gargoyle, he shook his head and then dropped his hands to hang at his sides. "Fine. But promise me you'll get a ward tattoo from Judy."

Anger's smoky scent dissipated as the smell of my confusion took over. I arched an eyebrow at him.

"It's a temporary tattoo that shields against mild injuries. If you're in another fire, for example, it will lessen burns. But it only works once, and it's not foolproof. Judy practiced the ward spell on me when I had to fly to the top of the lighthouse to change the bulb." His wings expanded slightly. "These aren't meant to take me that high, so the ward was a precaution that worked. When I—" He cleared his throat and paused. "I accidentally crushed the bulb and the glass cut me. But the ward prevented the cut from bleeding."

My lips parted and my brow pinched. "Are you okay? I thought your skin was tougher..." I didn't know how to word it. Sett looked invincible to me. Massive, muscular, always aware of his surroundings.

He understood my curiosity. "Stone skin cracks too. And sometimes I don't know my own strength." Something flickered over his face. I thought I knew Sett, but I'd never heard him say anything like that before. And for once, I smelled him. I smelled the wet soil of heavy rain mixed with the char of charred toast. What made Sett so sad and regretful? It was the only explanation he offered before he directed the conversation back to me. "You and all the pups should get the ward tattoo immediately. I'm going to warn Miss Raven and Judy about the second threat and recommend they leave town."

I narrowed my eyes. "You're going to encourage them to move?"

"They won't have to. Not if I can catch this creep."

On this, we agreed. The vandal was a certified creep, and it gave me the heebie jeebies to think they were among us this afternoon. "Won't they know Miss Raven and Judy aren't actually moving? It'll be obvious without a moving truck and boxes..."

A long breath blew through his nose and his jaw shifted side-to-side. "Yes. But my main objective is to keep them safe and alive. We'll do our best with the rest. Don't forget my deputy received a note too. He left, and his apartment hasn't been sabotaged."

Could that be because the deputy hadn't officially moved in yet? He temporarily rented from Mae while he waited to buy a home here. The month-to-month lease didn't exactly signal that he'd locked it down as a permanent residence. Maybe the vandal believed the deputy had truly relocated, and since the coroner's family lived out of town, it appeared he was officially gone too.

I kept the devil's advocate comment to myself. Sett was already on edge and bordering on overprotective. He'd tell me to run away and abandon the family I'd created here in Bewitcher's Beach. No way would I move away.

Sett stepped closer, our opposite shoulders nearly touching as he looked down at me. "You'll get the tattoo, right?"

Of course I'd get the tattoo, but the question aggravated like a buzzing fly in my ear. I gritted my teeth, but it only doubled the tension and soreness in my cheeks and throat. After the threats and Cliff's demands, Sett's suggestion tipped me over the edge like a leaning stack of VHS tapes in my arms. *Straw, meet camel's back.*

Finally, I craned my neck and met his eyes. Tenderness contrasted his tough, stony skin. All at once, the flame in my temper was doused with a splash of cool water. "I'll get the tattoo. Right now."

The edge of his mouth curled slightly. Did Sett Lawrence actually crack a smile? He said nothing as he brushed past me, careful not to bump my shoulder too hard. While he headed for The Oyster Inn, I turned my attention to the library.

Really, this was perfect timing. Since I couldn't visit Shadowvale Witch College, I wanted to talk with Judy about spells and prophecies and the magical book that was once housed in her library.

I supposed I could fit a magical tattoo into my visit as well.

BY THE TIME I retrieved the pups from a day of roller skating and made it back across town to the library, dusk had fallen. I tugged the hoodie off my waist and pulled it over my head. Clouds descended closer to the rooftops. If only they were fluffy and white rather than wispy and gray, the buildings would look snow-topped for the holidays.

Though werewolves were rarely affected by cold, we walked briskly to avoid the bone chill of the night. In our human forms, we didn't have thick fur coats to shield us from the frigid bite that came out when the sun retreated.

Closer to the beach, the wind grew stronger, blowing sand all the way up to the cobblestone outside the library. If we proceeded along the path, we'd end up on the shore, but we veered to the right and pushed through to the quiet comfort of the brick building.

The library stored hundreds of books, old and new. Many held rich histories regarding Bewitcher's Beach's magic and the pirates that camped here centuries before. Judy pivoted to greet us as we entered, her copper hair swishing over her shoulders.

With a frown, she squinted at us through glasses shaped in two black cat heads.

Halen barked at Dio, who had called him a loser, and Stevie loudly sang a song about how much she loved her pet Dungeness crab.

I cringed as Judy's sharp red gaze swept over the rowdy pack of pups. "I'm sorry."

Slowly and while whispering to herself, she raised a single finger to her lips before releasing a powerful *SHHH!* The children startled and obliged, falling silent. They quietly bounded off to their favorite corners of the library. Stevie found books on nature and animals while Dio dug out sports stories. Halen found joke books, and Jovi bounced between the science section and classic literature.

Facing Judy, I smiled. "Now that's some magic! I see you've been practicing. Can you teach me that?" My voice pitched louder than I'd intended, and she glared at me over the frame of her cat glasses.

In a calm but clear tone, she responded, gazing down at the box of rental records on her desk as she spoke. "I have no intention of teaching, even if *anyone* can learn basic magic. It has taken me many hours of meticulous study to accomplish even the most simple of spells. And seeing as I have witch ancestry, it is easier for me. Imagine how long it might take for someone without that heritage."

"Wait, was the shush really magic? I was kidding."

"Do I look like a woman who jokes?" Her red eyes flicked, eyeing me over the glasses again. "I learned the shushing spell because of that awful ghost. Cliff likes to come in here and complain that this building is an eyesore, and I was sick of it. The *hushed hex* is merely an encouragement for silence the way the smell of lavender inspires calm." A little grin brightened her shimmering face, and the creases of her smile lines buried the scattered freckles on her skin. "I figured I would explain it in a way that might relate to you with that nose of yours." Speaking of lavender, Judy told the truth. I could smell it sloughing off her like she was the plant itself. "I have my magic, and you have yours."

"Your magic is why I'm here." I shuffled closer, leaning my elbows on the tall desk. "A little gargoyle told me you've learned a guarding ward? Or—he called it a protection tattoo."

"That gargoyle is anything but little. And yes, you are correct. Are you in need of protection, Noema?"

"The not-so-little gargoyle seems to think so." I fingered the papers in the pocket of my hoodie. I'd folded both notes and carried them with me. Having them within reach provided a slice of comfort, as if clinging to the papers would somehow reveal clues.

"Oh?" Both her brows raised, crinkling her forehead. The black glasses slipped down her thin nose. "What for?"

I dropped my voice and leaned over the desk, hoping the kids wouldn't hear. "I was threatened too. This morning."

After a sharp breath, she removed her glasses and rubbed at the spot where they rested on her nose. "I take it you refuse to move as well?"

"That's right," I said. That was enough to convince her, and while I spoke, she produced a paintbrush and ink from beneath the desk. "Sett wants me to leave town until this is solved, but I don't feel comfortable leaving Mockbuster unattended."

Judy edged around the desk, using the paintbrush to point at the round table in the center of the library. I followed and sat across from her. Once she took a seat and set up the supplies, she motioned for me to hold out my hand. The brush's bristles tickled my knuckles with each stroke. Soon, an image formed in the paint, and a rounded shield covered the back of my hand. She glanced up at me in between strokes. "I thought you were planning a trip to Shadowvale. Don't you have a young ghost who works there that can watch over Mockbuster?"

"Bette? Yes, she helps out. But if the vandal tries to burn my shop like they did to Miss Raven's studio, Bette wouldn't be able to do much to stop it. It takes her almost a whole minute to solidify enough to even grab the phone."

"I suppose we all have our unique talents and weaknesses," Judy mused, eyes far off before she sucked in a breath and focused on the tattoo again. The shield was coming together nicely. A pretty piece of artwork. Too bad it wouldn't last long. There was so much I didn't know about magic. So much in *The Book of Prophecies* that I wished to learn.

"Can you tell more about the prophecies?" I asked, resisting the sudden urge to laugh as the paintbrush swirled too close to my wrist. She ignored my twitching and muttered a spell over it. The blue ink stained quickly, and the paint shimmered with her magic.

"Hmm." She sat back as the magical protection melted into my skin. While the ink dried, she called Halen over for his shield. He requested a green shield with a picture of the Teenage Mutant Ninja Turtles on it. Judy sighed but started mixing the yellow paint with the blue she'd used on me."What can I tell you about the spell book that you don't already know?"

"I know you read some of the spells before the witches took the grimoire to Shadowvale," I started. "I thought I could get your opinion on if the spells sound like they were written by the same author. I'm trying to narrow down who might have created the book and, if I am related to them, what identifying factors can I pinpoint? Does the writing seem like it was by someone older, or younger? Do the spells share a lot of the same skills or ingredients?"

Judy hummed. "I like your attention to detail." She sent Halen off, who retrieved Dio for his turn at the painting station.

"Attention to detail is all I have right now until I can get to Shadowvale and speak with the witches."

"If only they worked a little faster studying that book, we might not have lost Aerobics Alive," she said. She didn't acknowledge my questions, instead changing the subject to one on all of our minds. "With the protection spell reinstated, we'd be spared from wasting concern for such destruction. Then may we aim our attention at knowledge and wisdom where it belongs." She arched a pencil-thin eyebrow and raked her gaze over me. Dio's tattoo was finished quickly and she moved on to Stevie, who requested a red shield to match her favorite Power Ranger. "You know," Judy continued, "it's a good thing that you cannot make it to Shadowvale. Sure, you are linked to one of the prophecies, but is that truly more important than letting the skilled witches focus on what really matters? The protection spell?"

I wanted to bark back, but she wasn't wrong. The spell that guarded the whole of Bewitcher's Beach should take precedence over my little identity quest. Though she couldn't smell the aroma of earthy rain floating around me, she seemed to understand my disappointment.

After Stevie bounded off and the last pup sat down for his painting, Judy broke the silence. "To answer your original questions, the spells I have worked with are most certainly created by the same person. Though that's only speaking of the very easy charms. That's not to say the more complex magic or witch-only intentions are from the same creator. If I recall correctly, there were a good deal of the older spells that used snow or cold environments to enhance the enchantment. This differs from the sand used in the later spells. Also—"

The phone trilled from the wall behind the front desk. She

quickly swirled the paintbrush to finish a simple golden shield on Jovi's hand. He'd wanted one that resembled a police's badge. With the tattoos complete, she hopped to her feet and hurried to the phone. "Excuse me."

While she unhooked the cream phone, twisting the long, winding cord around her fingers, I admired decorations brightening the library. Christmas books adorned the shelves alongside porcelain figurines of snowmen, miniature faux pine trees, and cats in holiday sweaters. A santa hat was hooked on the edge of a stack of books, and tacked to the bookshelf was a leafy green garland that twinkled with tiny white lights.

Judy gasped and my attention snapped to her. "No!" With her palm to her throat, her eyes bulged as if seeing a horror I could not. "My house?"

The sharp screech of a siren rang out from somewhere in Bewitcher's Beach. My throat tightened with the feeling of the leash again, and my ears shot forward, peaking to catch the nuances from where the siren resonated. In sync, we whipped our attention to the front window, where flashing red lights whizzed by on the bumpy cobblestone.

The fire truck headed straight for Judy's neighborhood.

CHAPTER 7
ON FIRE

A POWERFUL STREAM of foamy water rained down on Judy's cottage. Wedged behind a thick wall of hedges, the cozy home was separated from the suburban-style neighborhood and the older houses on the beach. Judy's was the only one in the narrow field between the hedges and the fence that encircled the rows of residences.

Because of this location, the cottage was the envy of many Bewitcher's Beach residents. It was both private and close to the shops, the neighborhood walking paths, and the beach. Plus, the fixed rent that Mae offered on this particular property boosted its desirability.

A string of crisp white Christmas lights fell from a hook along the house's trim. The forceful stream of water knocked it out of place until the entire string tumbled into the bushes that lined the front porch.

Tears glistened in more eyes than just Judy's. Flickering flames reflected in Mae's watery gaze. Mayor Fitz and Hattie mirrored the general melancholy. Another small crowd had gathered, curious at the sound of the siren that alerted the town of another fire.

"What a shame," Hattie said, voice cracking. Her smooth blonde bob swished along the curve of her jaw as she shook her head and stared at the fire. Flames ate away at the white shingles on the cottage's open gable roof. "This house has been here longer than me. One of the original Bewitcher's Beach cottages and a real show-stealer compared to the other houses. When I saw the fire truck screeching in this direction, I just had to know if it was okay."

Mayor Fitz nodded, brow furrowed, though he kept his usual positive tone and held his head high. "I felt the same, Miss Hattie. Especially seeing as the fire was near my house."

A deafening crack split through the air, followed by splinters. The roof caved in over a small window in the front, but the flames were tamed now, beaten back by the heavy blast from the firehose.

I stole a glance at Judy whose shoulders pulled to the ground as if an invisible string dragged her down. At the edge of the crowd, she stood alone, wrapped in sadness. My heart ached for her as her cozy little home lost a room and a square of the roof.

I scooted closer to her where the scent of wet soil and rain hovered. Her sorrow was a cloud of earthy aromas. "I owe you," I began, knowing her pride wouldn't accept an offer of help any other way. Especially from someone like me. Someone she considered rowdy and disorganized. Though she wasn't exactly wrong...

Red glistened in her wet eyes as she blinked at me. It quickly dried up as she straightened, tough and proud. I continued, "You gave us all a shield, so let me show you my gratitude. Tell me how I can help. We'll clean up like we did for Miss Raven. Or—"

"No." She clipped. After a hard swallow, she tucked her thick red hair behind one ear and sniffed, collecting herself again. "No, thank you. I won't be staying here, so there is no need to rush a restoration."

I tilted my head, waiting for her to explain. Likely, Sett's suggestion combined with the fire had convinced her to leave. No doubt he called her with information about the second threat as soon as we'd parted ways. Judy was stubborn, though; I didn't expect her to listen to the vandal's demands.

As if reading my thoughts, her attention fixed on me and her eyebrows lifted. "Staying isn't worth risking the books. Whoever attacked my house might come after the library if they know how much time I spend there."

The library. Of course. Judy valued the collection of tomes and grimoires, fiction and nonfiction, textbooks and spell books, over all else. If she left town, effectively obeying the creep who wanted to control us, the library could be spared. Though it was no promise of safety. Still, after what happened to Aerobics Alive and all of Miss Raven's equipment, I couldn't blame Judy for the choice to leave. The arsonist made it clear. They would not stop. But to move away... "You won't *leave* leave, will you?"

Judy pursed her lips, a flash of judgment in her eyes. "Do you mean to ask if I will be moving out of town?" She didn't wait for me to confirm. "Unlike you, I have no qualms with relocation. If it is necessary to save the library, I will do whatever it takes. In any case, I prefer books over people. While I may miss a few faces, moving would be worth it."

I respected her loyalty to books. I loved movies almost as much. But to leave friends...to move away from your home? She was right about one thing. Unlike her, I refused to move, though she had a point. Would leaving appease the vandal long enough to keep a target off Mockbuster?

Could I even leave now? A vise gripped my heart at the thought of telling the kids we'd leave Grandmae and the home we'd decorated right before Christmas. Would our trip turn into a permanent move if Sett couldn't track down this criminal? Stevie would worry Santa couldn't find her if she didn't return to Bewitcher's Beach by Christmas Day. Halen would be devastated to skip cookies with his grandparents. Jovi and Dio would insist they weren't crying when they definitely would. My chest tightened, leaving me breathless. After all the pups had been through, losing their father and not knowing their extended family, I couldn't fathom breaking such news to them. Breaking their whole lives here and telling them they'd have to say goodbye to their school, their friends, and the stickers they decorated their room with. Those Spiderman and Power Rangers decals were never coming off the wall.

Silence fell between us until Judy drew a sharp breath. "I'd like to request one small favor."

"Anything."

"I plan to pack up and leave as soon as I'm cleared to go inside. That means the library will be closed indefinitely. Please, have that studious son of yours monitor it for me."

"Jovi?" I asked, referring to my boy who loved to read. He was the quintessential bookworm with his thick-framed glasses and brain full of endless trivia and knowledge.

"I know the sheriff will take care of it, but he doesn't love books as much as your boy." She didn't call him by name because Judy kept everyone at arm's length. The lack of personable details indicated she didn't care to learn more about the people around her. Why, I didn't know. "I assume you will not be leaving town." Apparently, she knew *me* well enough. "And if I must relocate permanently—"

"You won't have to. Sett will stop the arsonist."

For once, Judy didn't snap at me for interrupting her. She didn't correct me either, only peered at me through narrowed eyes. The hint of a smile twitched at her lips, and the smell of hope swirled around her. The tangy sweetness of key lime pie lifted my spirits. "Sett will stop them? Or you will?"

I bit my tongue before admitting she knew me better than I knew myself. Judy and I weren't exactly close friends. My love for movies utterly bewildered her, and she took offense to the "crude form of media." But we'd built an alliance over the past couple of weeks, and Judy was astute. Not that I was exactly secretive about my commitment to defend Bewitcher's Beach.

She leaned in, voice low. "If I'm being honest, I'm relieved to hear you're on the case. Sett's overworked and underpaid. He simply cannot be in two places at once, and as little as you read—" She paused to release a forceful breath. When she spoke again, the judgment lacing her voice tempered. "As little as you read, history suggests you're willing to do what it takes to secure every part of this town." Her red eyes flashed, possibly with the memory of my less-than-legal approach to tracking criminals. I was impatient, sure, but at least it was for a good cause. And I'd gotten better at thinking before I act. Sometimes.

Once the flames were finally gone, the fire marshal offered to walk Judy inside so she could pack essentials. Judy obliged, following her a few steps before she paused and faced me. "One more favor. Catch the weasel who did this, and when you give them a fist in the nose, tell them it's from the librarian."

I tried to suppress my grin but those words coming from Judy's mouth and the suggestive fist were too much. I smirked. Glancing around, I quickly covered my mouth so nobody witnessed me smiling in front of a destroyed home.

"I'll track them down," I promised. Judy deserved the right to return. And Jovi, as well as the rest of the kids and readers in Bewitcher's Beach, deserved a knowledgeable librarian. Judy shook her fist and mimed a punch through the air before turning to follow the fire marshal.

If I caught this creep, like Judy requested, I wouldn't be forced to break bad news to the pups. Courage bolstered me, igniting with energy in my fast-beating heart. I wouldn't ruin Christmas by leaving Grandmae. And now, I had a promise to keep.

I shuffled back to the crowd just as Mayor Fitz addressed everyone. "There is one bit of good news. The builder remodeling my house took inspiration from this cottage's bay windows and arched doorways. In my house, memories of these designs will live on."

"Goodness me," Mae said. "The cottage is still standing, Fitz. " Mae stooped to set her poodle on the ground and face the mayor. A bit of smoke wafted from the half-dragon's nose. "You can see the only room that burned is the laundry alcove."

"You're absolutely right, Mae, and what you said embodies the mission of my campaign." Though he stood a head shorter than the half-dragon, the squat man reached her shoulder to give her a grateful pat.

"I merely said the cottage is still standing—"

"Exactly!" Mayor Fitz beamed, cheeks rosy. His bald head shone even brighter as a nearby lamp post flicked on. "Always look at the bright side." He puffed out his chest and offered a warm smile to Mae then passed his gaze to each of us. "My opponent, Dr. Pitt, is a great man. But he is not here today to uplift us, is he?" Dr. Pitt didn't take the extra time to campaign that Mayor Fitz did. But it didn't affect his ratings in *The Bewitcher's Beach Gazette* surveys. People personally trusted the doctor. But they believed in Fitz too, which would make for a close race at the polls on voting day. "Bewitcher's Beach needs one more term with a dedicated, experienced, and *uplifting* leader. Such incidents as these have risen lately without the protection spell. So it is my promise as your mayor now and next term that I will use my personal time and experience as a former volunteer police officer to safeguard our town. I'll shine a light on all the positives until there is no room left for the darker times."

"How does that help those of us who have already died?" An angry voice bellowed from the back. Hattie and I whirled around, but Mae only rolled her eyes, having already recognized the voice.

It dawned on me before I found the frosted tips. Cliff was here to cause trouble. The apparition flickered until he filled in enough to look like a full ghost. He solidified and fiddled with an object in one hand. Whatever it was reflected the sun like Mayor Fitz's shiny head.

Before I could concentrate on my own thoughts, his raspy voice yanked me from my mind. "This isn't far from the house I haunt. What if mine burns to a crisp too?" Didn't he want everything tied to his investigation burned to a crisp anyway? He flung his hands up in mock surrender, the anger causing his apparition to blink in and out like a television with a bad connection. "It's all I have left here! It would have been nice if you'd prevented the crime before it occurred instead of making empty promises."

I glanced from the ghost to Mayor Fitz, who didn't so much as stutter. Instead, his ever-present grin widened, and his pink cheeks reminded me of jolly old Santa Claus. Until the rancid smell of rotten fish ruined the image. Mayor Fitz likely struggled with an internal battle of guilt over Cliff's murder. Crime *was* rising in Bewitcher's Beach, making his promise trickier to keep. But he had Sett's expertise and Judy's temporary warding skills, at least when she returned. Even Mae's newspaper reports supported him. Each of us played a role in keeping the town safe, and Fitz was a talented leader when it came to encouraging and inspiring us to be a team.

"That is certainly an insightful suggestion, Mr. Conflick."

Fitz strode through the crowd toward the flickering ghost. Cliff sneered and folded his arms, snubbing the mayor's attempt at a handshake. Of course his hand would pass through the apparition of the hand anyway, but it was the thought that counted—at least that was what I assumed Fitz would say. Always look on the bright side, even as buildings burned down. "Cliff here has inspired an idea. If I'm reelected, I will make it my priority to employ a seer on Bewitcher's Beach's First Responders team. A seer would certainly be the first to respond!" He thrust a finger in the air and smiled at a few of the surrounding people who rewarded his joke with scattered chuckles. He focused his attention on Cliff again. "Thank you, Mr. Conflick. What a wonderful proposal from a smart man."

Cliff huffed but he didn't argue. Fitz successfully thwarted the indignant ghost's abrasive complaints with praise. For now anyway.

"A seer?" I repeated. It truly was a wonderful idea. Though I'd heard witches with such power were few and far between. Only one was mentioned in the prophecy. If I dug deeper into my connection to the prophecy, would I find a seer in my own family line? It was a thought for another time.

The crowd dispersed after the fire was tamed, leaving only Mae, Sett, and the fire marshal, who spoke with Judy. Judy showered her with gratitude for saving most of the house. The fire wrecked the laundry alcove, the roof above that, and a corner of the kitchen, but her miniature library in the living room was spared of damage.

Sett addressed Mae. "I recommend you and Judy contact the insurance company as soon as the fire marshal finishes assessing the total damage."

"How long will that be?" Mae asked.

"Soon," he said, his voice gravelly after inhaling a bit of smoke. "Mae, do you know of anyone who would target your rentals? Anyone who might be angry at you for raising the cost of their rent? Or maybe you offended them with something you wrote in *The Bewitcher's Beach Gazette*?"

A pit opened in my stomach, sickened by a reminder of the threats. Or maybe it was hunger. Whatever triggered it, the gnawing sensation only grew with Mae's reaction.

Her mouth dropped open, and the sting of ammonia mixed with pineapple pizza's scent. "How dare you suggest such a thing?"

He raised his hand, pen tucked between his fingers. "I meant no offense."

"Didn't I hear you already have a suspect? Triton told me he saw a visitor outside Aerobics Alive around the time of the fire. Zed and his son, was it?" Sett opened his mouth, but Mae wouldn't let him get a word in. "Anyway, no, I didn't raise anyone's rent. And for your information, I never report anything that I don't first receive permission from the source to share." She ended with a little defiant *humph*.

"That's good to hear." He scribbled it on his notepad. "Excuse me while I look around and see what I can shake out. In the meantime, you stay safe." His gaze was on me. Again.

"Of course," I said cheerfully. But my promise didn't convince him. Sett's brow quirked and he pursed his lips, eyes narrowed as he considered whether to believe me. I crossed my arms, and the smoky smell of my exasperation swelled in the cramped space between us. Sure, it was true he'd warned me to be careful before. And sure, I'd wound up involved in two murder investigations. But if a bit of trouble was the price I had to pay to help keep my pups' home safe, I would do it again. A thought dawned on me, and I hurried to follow him. "Is this visitor Mae mentioned a concern?"

Sett blew out a breath that coiled into mist. With his hands tucked into his coat pocket, he stomped toward the building, knowing I'd follow at his heels until I received an answer. "They're not concrete suspects," he said. "Zed and his son were merely seen nearby. Taking a walk isn't a crime. The guy has no motive. He's a carpenter here to remodel Mayor Fitz's house." Reed hung around the studio, but I didn't know what time he left.

Sett fell silent as he assessed the building. Now that the sun was down, even if it was mostly hidden behind clouds today, a chill settled over Bewitcher's Beach. The shore breeze swept through town, salty and cold as it ruffled the fur on my peaked wolf ears.

I followed as he rounded to the back of the house, looking up and down at the charred wall. Back here, we were sheltered from the wind. "And you're sure he's not a hunter?" I asked, referring to the rogue people who disliked supernaturals. Hunters claimed to keep humans safe from werewolves and vampires. Of course, it was illegal to hurt anyone, and I'd never seen a hunter. Supernatural-dense regions like Bewitcher's Beach were mostly secure.

Sett chuckled. "I don't think someone married to a gargoyle and with a half-gargoyle son would be a hunter. Since Zed and Reed were seen nearby after the fire broke out, I had to question them. Mae's the one to call them suspects."

The ashy skin and hunched back... Suddenly Reed's characteristics made sense. He buried his gargoyle wings beneath his clothing.

The image in my mind's eye dissolved as I reached out and brushed my fingers through a window frame. The glass was gone, having been blown out by the heat of the fire. But the frame remained intact, and the wall stood strong since it wasn't near the affected area. "This is so sad. Who could do such a thing?"

"Some people vandalize just for the thrill of it." He examined a drain pipe before his gaze landed on me. "I've yet to establish a specific connection between those of you who received threats. The result leads me to question a wide range of people. Lack of solid leads is what prompts me to encourage each targeted victim to take time away from Bewitcher's Beach."

A chill trickled through me, and a sudden urge to shift into my wolf form had me biting back a howl. We walked back to the other side of the house where the damage was the worst. The laundry alcove had been devoured, but the washing and drying machines remained untouched.

A wooden plank that didn't match the rest of the house was tacked onto the wall just above the ground. It was ill-fitting, not entirely covering the narrow opening that resembled an over-sized dog door. The rectangle was about five times the size of the tiny opening I'd cut into the wall between Mockbuster and Everland Theater so Squeaks could come and go as he pleased. This was bigger than the doggie door Mae had for Babette too. "What's that?"

Sett tilted his head, eyeing the boarded opening. "That's a wildlife invitation. They're called Creature Cutouts. All of the older homes in Bewitcher's Beach included them because people used to invite wildlife into their homes as familiars or to make trades. Any animals with traces of magic were welcome."

"Huh. I guess you've been visiting the library more than me lately."

He shook his head. "I only know because my house has one."

When I stepped closer, a harsh and acrid odor stung my nose and forced a cough from my throat. I sniffed again, discerning the strange smell from the lingering smoke of the fire. Did it come from an emotion? My gaze drifted to Sett, who was scribbling another note. "Are you mad at me?" The question blurted from me before I could think it through. Why would he be mad? But the smell of smoke always came from anger. This was distinct from the fire, spicy and sweet and with a hint of something else.

Sett cocked his head. "What? No."

I crouched, zeroing in on the source of the odor. "Do you smell that?" I brushed my hand over the rubble. The soot left black marks on my fingertips. Like a game of "hot or cold," I sniffed along the trail, following it several paces away from the cottage. A small cylinder of crumbled paper lay in the grass. My breath hitched at the sight of another note, this one coiled. I stooped and plucked the paper wrapping from the ground and determined it was far too small to be any kind of note, rather the wrapping of a cigarette. I brought it to my nose and sniffed. The spicy nicotine made me sneeze as it soured my stomach.

"What is it?" Sett asked.

"A butt," I said, holding the piece of the cigarette aloft.

"A butt?" Footsteps stormed closer, and the shadow of Sett's body cast over me. "Oh, a cigarette."

"Smoking cigarettes..." I breathed as threads came together in my mind. Wasn't I supposed to sniff out the truth from a boy who smoked cigarettes and donned skull tattoos for Hattie's sake? My head spun as I shot to my feet. "You said Reed and Zed were near Aerobics Alive before the fire?" When had Reed slipped inside to visit with Bette? And when did he leave? I was too focused on not falling down to recall the details. Sett nodded faintly as he scrutinized me and the cigarette butt pinched between my fingers. "I don't know if this helps your investigation, but Hattie told me Reed smokes. She wanted me to vet him. I was supposed to sniff out if he was lying during an interview with her before Bette spent time with him."

Sett pulled a plastic evidence bag from his coat pocket and

instructed me to drop the cigarette butt inside. "Looks like I need to talk with Zed again."

What if Reed had heard of Hattie's plan and wanted to frighten me with the second note? Of course, that didn't explain the other threats.

The pieces didn't form a puzzle. All I wanted was to see the bigger picture before my time was up and Mockbuster burned. Or worse.

CHAPTER 8
BURNT OUT

A NIGHT SPENT LYING awake and trying to piece the puzzle together left me dragging at Aerobics Alive the next morning. Regulars showed up early to set up what was left of the studio.

This was one puzzle we *could* solve. The pieces were simple: support Miss Raven by attending her last class before she left town, and keep an eye on the building for her.

We banded around her like a shield. Or rather, an extra dozen sets of eyes. Both real and mechanical. Precautions were set up with extra security cameras donated from Miss Chanel's clothing boutique. Just for today, Triton closed his shop so he could post up outside Aerobics Alive like a security guard. Wallace joined him, and they stood with their arms crossed, looking as tough as possible.

I smiled at them both as I hurried to the class.

Celeste held the door open for me and then slipped inside behind me. Delicious scents slammed me the second I stepped through the door. The aroma of key lime pie hung in the air, nearly as palpable as if I was breathing the fluffy meringue.

Returning to Aerobics Alive fostered a sense of hope. Even if it was Miss Raven's last class.

"Welcome, welcome!" She said, beaming. Her fluffy pony-tail swept back and forth like a windshield wiper as she paced the studio, giving hugs and patting backs.

Since clean up was complete and the investigators had evidence already tagged and stored for safekeeping, classes resumed inside the partial building. Even without a full roof and two half-standing walls, the structure was better than the high fee The Oyster Inn charged to use the meeting hall. Soon, we'd all pitch in and rebuild what had been lost.

Mae bought Miss Raven a new boombox, and Crow brought the entire CD collection that was once used at Roller Shakes before the sound system was updated. Celeste donated cash to replace destroyed equipment. Gradually, we restored the details that made Aerobics Alive Miss Raven's unique sanctuary.

I selected a repaired platform and placed it on the ground in front of me. Though the studio's wooden floor burned to half the size, we crammed inside for a modified workout. Hopefully, we didn't kick each other off our platforms. It'd be a tight squeeze with every hop, skip, and jump.

With Mae and her poodle to my right and Crow set up on my left, it was like the fire never happened. He even showed up in the slashed shirt. When he caught me eyeing it, he gave me a smirk and a wink. "My stylist told me it's pretty fly. But don't worry, I'll change for our date."

I'd forgotten about our plans. Anticipation for a night alone with Crow left me flushed. But could I risk an evening away from Mockbuster?

Before I could respond, Miss Raven stole my attention away. The petite reaper smoothed her palm over her long, black ponytail, drawing it over her shoulder as she spoke. "What would I do without each and every one of you?"

"You'd miss our sweaty faces every morning. That's for darn sure," Mae said. Others nodded along, and the poodle yapped her agreement until she hopped off Mae's platform and headed for a bird on the cobblestone. "Babette!" she screeched and bustled after the dog, who wouldn't stay put within the open structure.

When Miss Raven's eyes grew misty, mine stung. "I just wanted to say thank you for all the help you've offered." I scanned the room, grateful for all the people who made Bewitcher's Beach a home—a family. Though we weren't related, and I'd certainly never quite fit in with the women in their matching spandex, I was a part of their community. I wanted to help more, but supporting four pups as a single mom made donations off the table, and I didn't think a movie collection would be as practical as the music contribution.

I *did* know a little about fixing up and redecorating. Since Mockbuster was a mess when I took it over, I'd done as much renovation as I knew how. Plus, I had strong legs and usually plenty of werewolf energy to offer. According to Mae, the insurance company dragged when returning a financial quote that allowed restoration to start. But we could bypass the wait.

"So when do we start rebuilding?" I asked. "Bette covers Mockbuster when I'm not there. So I can get away to move some wood or hammer a nail during the day while the pups are in school. We can work on it while you're away."

"Rebuild?" Miss Raven's sharp brows spiked and she pursed her lips. Another flood of tears swam in her navy blue eyes. "I don't know what to say." Her voice cracked as she pivoted on her step platform. She scanned the destroyed section behind her, and then shook her head. "It's too much work."

"Many hands make light work," I said, a cliche—though true—I'd heard from Mayor Fitz more than once.

"What are we talking about?" Mae returned with the fluffy pooch in her arms, breathless and glistening with beads of sweat from the chase. When Miss Raven filled her in, Mae interrupted. "No, no. As valiant and kindhearted as you all are, I've already spoken with the contractor remodeling Mayor Fitz's house. He's willing to give us a good deal in case there's anything the insurance won't cover. In fact, he's supposed to drop by this morning and assess the structure for an estimate."

"This is the best option," Miss Raven said, resolved. She brushed her fluffy bangs from her forehead and took a deep breath. "As a retired reaper, I take death more seriously than the average person. I'll not have you forcing me out of retirement because you put yourselves at risk to rebuild this place. More than one of you have tripped over a step platform. I don't want to see you climbing ladders for my sake."

The dark humor sparked scattering chuckles. But the joke's acknowledgment of the second note—the added threat—tightened my throat and cut off a chuckle. The risk she referred to was more than our lack of coordination. Of that, I was sure.

I tried to make light of it, shaking off the ominous weight. "I'd crack like Humpty Dumpty if I tried to scale a ladder."

Mae leaned toward us. "If anything actually happened to us, Crow would help with the reaping."

My mouth dropped open. Very few people knew Crow was a reaper since he preferred to keep his Calling under wraps. Mae's slip just let the Calling out of the bag because, as quietly as she'd intended to speak, Mae only had one volume: loud.

I shot him a look, examining his blanched face. Celeste's eyes switched from Crow to Mae as she whispered to the woman in the high-top sneakers beside her. *Oh no...* By tonight, the whole town would know about Crow.

The whispering clued Mae in, and she slapped her hand to her mouth. "I wasn't thinking. I'm so sorry." Regret's odor sloughed off of her as clearly as if she'd become the piece of charred toast that she smelled like. "I forgot you're a very private guy."

Crow cleared his throat and gave her a reassuring nod. "It's okay. It's really not a secret anymore." Even though his stalker was behind bars, I often caught him looking over his shoulder in large crowds or on dark nights. I couldn't blame him for keeping his Calling quiet. As it turned out, people didn't exactly love the guy who had to whisk away the spirits of their passed loved ones. Their anger was misguided, but grief wasn't always logical.

Before I could ask if he was okay, Miss Raven began the count. *Five, six, seven, eight!* I resolved to check in with Crow after class. I needed to postpone the date we'd scheduled for tonight anyway. With my promise to Judy hovering and Christmas on the horizon, I couldn't rationalize a night of relaxing. Instead, we could grab a bite at Roller Shakes while I went over the leads. If Sett couldn't find a targeted connection between the deputy, Miss Raven, Judy, and I, could I?

"Put your heart into it!" Miss Raven interrupted my thoughts. "Make that ticker work harder and grow stronger and live longer!"

We stepped up on number one, kicked out on two, and clapped our hands over our heads on three, then repeated the routine on the other side, falling into a rhythm with the music. *Cotton Eye Joe* blasted from the new boombox. Worry over Reed and Zed, cigarettes and threatening notes, angry ghosts and Rick Astley songs, melted away as if dripping off of me with the sweat.

When we paused for a water break, I took the time to check

in with Crow. He assured me he was fine, so I broke the news about our date.

"Counter offer," he said. "You can go over leads with me *while* on the date." I quietly considered this, working on the whole "think before you act" thing. "If that's too much, I get it. But the date is here in town, so you won't have to venture far from Mockbuster and it won't take too much of your time. Also, bonus suggestion. If you want to make a suspect board after, I have string and push pins at my house. "

A smile pulled at my lips. I'd told him about my promise to Judy, and he knew of my unspoken commitment to keep Bewitcher's Beach a charming and secure home for my kids. Maybe a break was what I needed. I certainly needed breaks during the workout. If step aerobics taught me anything, it was to take a breath. Or to take an evening clearing my head so I didn't have another night of tossing and turning. "Push pins? Count me in."

The second half of the workout ramped up in intensity, and I almost didn't finish. As we blew out a final breath and Miss Raven sent us off with her motto "Your workout today will keep the reaper away," I spotted two men approaching the open building. The blond man with a scruffy five o'clock shadow carried a notepad under one arm and walked with his other hand stuffed into scuffed jeans. He resembled Bruce Willis, and his son mirrored him. Though the boy trailing behind him, had dyed his spiked hair black and green, clearly setting himself apart from his father.

I wandered to the front of the studio to grab a bottle of cleaner. Spritzing some onto a rag, I eyed Zed and Reed as they stopped outside. A hulking figure marched up behind them. Sett cleared his throat and addressed Zed, reintroducing himself and the need for more questions.

Zed sniffed. "Sure. I don't know how I can be of any help."

"Everything helps," Sett said, pulling out his spiral-bound notebook. I sauntered back to my step platform, keeping my ears alert to catch the investigation interview. "Remind me what your business is here in Bewitcher's Beach."

"I'm a contractor working on a remodel."

I wiped the rag across the step platform and then scrubbed down the dumbbells I used. Crow bid me goodbye as everyone finished putting equipment away. They filed out one-by-one, ready to open their businesses, start their days, or take a shower. Shuffling and conversation drowned Zed's answers. I lingered, dragging the rag over every edge of the small hand weights until the studio was almost empty.

"Yes," Zed said, waving his hand toward the building. "I'll be working on this one too. I'm a businessman. Of course I hope to pick up more projects while I'm here."

"And your son is an assistant?"

"The best. Takes after his old man." Zed ruffled his son's mohawk, earning a death glare. Reed huffed and ducked away from his dad.

A shadow cast over me, and I craned my neck to see Miss Raven shooing me away. "I'll put these away, Noema. You've done more than enough. Run along and relax before those pups are out of school. Lack of rest brings the reaper, you know?"

Miss Raven had a way of telling me what to do that made me want to listen. I nodded obediently and hurried out of Aerobics Alive.

CHAPTER 9
WREATH IT AND WEEP

AS I WALKED BACK to Mockbuster, sights set on the dark windows, Miss Raven's recommendation hovered in the back of my mind. Like an itch on my spine that I couldn't reach in wolf form.

Get some relaxation? It felt like a joke. Scattered clues crowded my mind. Images of the gasoline the culprit used to start fires and discarded cigarettes haunted me.

Footsteps thumped behind me. I glanced over my shoulder, ears folded back. The green and black mohawk ducked and rose as Reed stalked behind me, quickly gaining pace. I could only hope Hattie's idea for us to interrogate him didn't piss him off.

Though it was broad daylight and in the middle of town, the fact that he matched my movements step-for-step left my skin prickling. Goosebumps popped up along my arms, and claws extended from my fingernails. Any closer and I'd become all fur and fangs before he took another step. If Reed tried to intimidate me, my bark should scare him enough that I wouldn't have to bite. Wolfing out wasn't the answer to all my solutions, but baring my fangs was an easy defense mechanism.

A ghost manifested behind Mockbuster's glass walls. For a second, I feared I'd be sandwiched between the stalking young man and an angry apparition, but Cliff wasn't the wispy figure in the window. Bette's strawberry hair floated behind her as she surged toward the open sign and flicked the light on, materializing solidly enough to hold the dangling rope chain.

When I dodged across the street and pulled the door open, the ghost beamed with a dazzling white smile. It wasn't me her dreamy eyes fell on. Reed walked in after me with a smug curl to his lips.

"Hey babe," he said to Bette, voice low and eyes flickering in my direction.

The couple sauntered away into the far aisle of family films, and I busied myself by booting up the desktop computer. Tidying the front desk, I swept a stack of rental cases in the bin to organize later. The internet's dial signal squealed as the computer's internet modem tried connecting online. I stared at the spinning hourglass symbol on the screen, only occasionally glancing at Reed and Bette.

"So did your mom get off our case yet?" he asked,

Bette hugged herself, shrugging one shoulder. "Not really. But what she doesn't know can't hurt her."

Bette! Did she forget she was in the presence of a werewolf? I often overheard more than I wanted.

"I like the sound of that," he said with a snicker. "Well, I gotta jet. My old man picked up another project, so we'll be here longer. When I get the extra cash, we can catch a movie in the next town over or somethin'."

"Totally."

Reed shuffled halfway to the exit, stopping only to snatch a horror movie from an endcap and snort at the spooky cover. Apparently to him, the clown on Stephen King's *IT* was more amusing than terrifying. He tossed it back on the shelf, sideways, and then shoved through the door, the bell chiming in his absence.

Before Bette could phase through the wall of new releases and disappear into Everland Theater, I edged around the desk and called out a thank you for opening the shop.

Bette spun around and surged forward, glowing with pink cheeks. "You're not going to tell my mom about Reed dropping by, are you?"

"Bette, it's not my business what you do, but it *is* hers. You should tell her."

Her shoulders sagged. "Then she'll interrogate him like a criminal!"

Hopefully, Hattie was wrong about him being a criminal. But he *was* witnessed near a crime, and it didn't look promising that his father's business was struggling. "You need to be careful, Bette. He's a stranger."

"Not to me!"

I put my hand on my hip, channeling the quintessential mother in sitcoms like *Home Improvement* or *Step by Step*. "What do you really know about him?"

"He's cooler than any guy who's ever lived in Bewitcher's Beach, that's for sure," Bette said, dreamily fawning over how easily Reed made her laugh.

"What else?"

While she talked, I multitasked by straightening cock-eyed movie cases and returning lost tapes to their correct sections. Bette followed, floating in my wake. I'd lost one stalker only to gain a shadow. But I loved Bette as if she were my own daughter, which made it harder to accept that she was dating a boy involved in an active investigation. "Where are they from?"

She lifted her shoulder and dropped it limply. "Not totally sure. He's here with his dad who's working on a remodel. He said business was slow before working with the mayor."

"Working with the mayor? Do you mean on his house, or something else?"

Another shrug. "No idea. Something about giving Bewitcher's Beach a facelift. That's what Reed said his dad calls it. He said they scored when they made connections with the mayor because the mayor is campaigning and making all kinds of promises to bring the town up to date."

A facelift for the older buildings? That'd certainly give the contractor more business. But the longer they stayed in Bewitcher's Beach, the more likely Zed would learn most of us didn't want to change the original structures. Many sites were even considered historical. Had they resorted to arson to push the updating project? If Mayor Fitz knew, he'd certainly rethink working with them. Though a bit of remodeling could draw more tourists into town and that *was* tempting for many of us small business owners. I couldn't fault Mayor Fitz or even Zed for wanting to give us that.

"Reed makes more money than anyone else his age," Bette continued. "He's responsible with it too. He bought his own car, and he's even saving for a spoiler to upgrade it."

"Did you happen to see Reed last night?"

Bette hummed, her head cocked. "Umm, no. Oh! I remember why. Reed said he had to help his dad with something. That's why I didn't sneak out—I mean, seek. Him. Out... last night."

"Right."

Help his dad? I sure hoped it wasn't with arson. For Bette's sake. But the suspect list seemed low, and Sett didn't include Cliff since he had no proof the insufferable ghost was anywhere near Aerobics Alive before the fire. Who else had the motive to sabotage two buildings in historic Bewitcher's Beach? Reed's innocence withered the longer I thought about it.

I gave myself a little shake as I panned the length of the

video shop. I loved the soft gray carpet, the bright yellow wall of new releases, and the unique essence of buttery popcorn, plastic cases, and hints of candy. If Mockbuster was next on the charring block, my heart might burn right along with it.

THREE HOURS LATER, I closed and locked the shop. The scent of my excitement filled my nose with the sweetness of banana cream pie. Tonight's date would be a reprieve from the heaviness dropped on us by the threats.

Everything fell in line. For now. Bette promised to be honest with her mom. The kids were crafting homemade Christmas cards with Mae and Wallace. And I had a date. An event, Crow insisted, that'd allow me to keep an eye on Mockbuster.

I followed him from Roller Shakes across the cobblestone and to the field in the center of town. He took my hand, and we jogged to get out of a bicyclist's way.

"We're not going ice skating, are we?" I pointed at the rink where skaters slipped and couples leaned on one another. "Jingle Bell Rock" blared from the speakers set up around the rink.

Christmas lights twinkled in his eyes, and his mouth curled into a smirk. "From roller skating to ice skating."

"Do you have any idea how clumsy I am?"

"I do. But I'm here to catch you."

With a laugh, I said, "I thought we said we'd be on the ground together."

"That's during step aerobics. Since taking over Roller Shakes, I've acquired a new skill. Prepare to be impressed." He paid the teenage ticket-taker, and I picked out a pair of brown ice skates from a shelf. He went for the hockey style skates.

Crow pulled on his skates, promptly hopped off the bench, and stepped onto the ice. He skated a quick circle, bypassing kids and the other couples. With a spray of ice, he slid to a sudden stop back at the entrance and offered his arm. From unpredictable to the perfect gentleman in less than a minute. That was Crow.

I accepted his arm and, with shaking legs, stepped onto the slick surface. My legs did not obey. All wiry muscle, Crow easily held me in place while my feet slid in opposite directions. I yelped and clung to him like he was a ledge and I'd fall a hundred feet.

"Steady," he said. Once I got my feet under me where they belonged, we shuffled forward. I gripped his elbow, puffing with careful breaths.

After a few moments, we picked up speed. The sensation of flying sent shivers of adrenaline up and down my arms and legs. As we circled around several times, he listened to me talk about holiday traditions. About Mae and Wallace. About my promise to Judy and why it meant so much for me to stay living in Bewitcher's Beach. About the tapes I needed to torch for Cliff's sake—only I couldn't bring myself to do it yet. I glanced at Mockbuster once or twice. Just to be sure it wasn't on fire or spray painted with Xs.

After an hour, I shuffled less and used the edge of the blade to push into short bursts of speed. Though with each push, I tightened my grip on him. He instructed me to reach for my knees when it felt slippery. It worked, and I beamed up at him. "I think I'm getting it."

"Good, because I'm letting you go."

"Oh heck no—"

He let go.

I screeched, arms flailing like a cat falling from a tree. Unlike a cat, canines didn't always land on their feet. My claws extended and fur sprouted over my skin. The sudden threat had me shifting into my safest form.

A lithe arm slipped around my lower back and, as promised, Crow caught me mid-fall. And mid-shift. Since I didn't fully shift, my claws and fur receded as quickly as they came.

His mouth crooked in a sideways smile. When he straightened both of us, I socked him lightly on the shoulder. "Don't do that!" My goofy grin surely betrayed my words. The combination of ice skating, holding hands under the Christmas lights, and even the clumsy slipping and sliding had me feeling young and... not in love. I didn't exude the scent of vanilla around Crow. But adrenaline blended with excitement, and pure joy smelled pretty darn close. Maybe like syrup.

My stomach grumbled at the thought. "You mentioned something about push pins. Are there snacks involved in this suspect board craft?" It was my turn to smirk and wiggle my brows at him.

He leaned against the short wall surrounding the rink and crossed his arm. "I might have wine at the house, but I don't stock a lot of groceries."

"Oh that's fine." I quickly waved my question away. Not everybody enjoyed cooking. I'd simply been around Sett too much. He was always trying to feed me. My stomach countered with a bubbling growl. Apparently, it didn't get the message that the man before me was a different handsome friend. "What about grabbing a to-go bag from Roller Shakes?"

"Count me in."

We skated half a dozen more rounds before I eased off the ice and tugged off my skates. I ran for a quick check-in with Hattie, who'd promised to watch Mockbuster during my date.

I'll call Sett if there's anything suspicious. You need to get Crow out of your system. Whatever that meant. But with Hattie haunting it, I felt comfortable enough to leave Mockbuster for an hour or two. And in an emergency, I could shift to my wolf form and be there in a flash.

So Crow and I headed for his house after stopping by Roller Shakes for a to-go bag of greasy french fries. Munching as we walked, I admired the new decorations that popped up. Each day, shop owners hung more bows and lights. We were a competitive lot. Or maybe they simply wanted to add more to their Christmas collections.

Echoes of "I'll Be Home For Christmas" faded the farther we drew from the rink.

Crow bunched the empty fry bag in one hand and took my hand into his other. A thrill shuddered through me as he lifted my hand for an innocent kiss. At this rate, and with wine, I pictured a *less* innocent kiss. A twinge in my stomach sent it grumbling again, and all thoughts of a kiss vanished. That much grease on an empty stomach didn't do me any favors. I drew in a deep whiff of fresh air to settle my stomach.

Away from the rink, the crash of waves drowned the distant jingle of Christmas songs. A dull wind swept through town as we wound past the coroner's office and the police station. Behind that, a batch of one-room cottages stood in a row. These five houses had views of both the beach and the forest that stretched along the northwestern side of Bewitcher's Beach's border. With holiday adornments, the tiny homes reminded me of gingerbread houses. Wreaths on the front doors looked like green gumdrops from a distance.

As we approached, I noticed something white tacked to the wreath on the house in front of us. Crow's house. Pepperminty curiosity rivaled the salty scent carried up by the breeze. We drew closer, and I squinted at the paper flapping in the wind.

"Crow..." I glanced at him. *Are you thinking what I'm thinking?*

He unlaced his fingers from my hand and stepped onto the porch, eyes glued to the paper. Peppermint faded to the scent of ammonia. Both my and Crow's worry and fear interlaced like our hands.

He snatched the paper from where it was taped to the wreath's bristles. In the dim yellow light of the porch bulb, he went white. Nausea from the greasy snack shifted to a gnawing pit in my stomach where my heart dropped.

He read aloud. *"Abandon the premises for your own safety. Vacate Bewitcher's Beach and you'll be spared."* Tense silence only broke with another crash of waves. His eyes, darker than ever, ticked up and landed on me through the hair that'd dipped into his face. A frown twisted his mouth. "I'm sorry, Noema. But I think I have to leave."

For a guy who had to run from a threat on his life before, I didn't blame him one bit. But it hurt all the same.

CHAPTER 10
BLAZING A TRAIL

THE DAY after saying goodbye to Crow—at least for now—I followed up on my promise. Not the promise I made Judy, but the one I'd said to Crow when he packed a suitcase.

While he took a hotel room in Carmel-by-the-sea, I swore on the fate of Mockbuster that I'd take time to think. I'd think about the picture the clues created, fully, before tracking a suspect. I'd think, I'd relax, I'd eat cherry snowball cookies. Then and only then, and with a belly full of sugar, would I act.

So this morning, I shook off the heebie jeebies with Mae and Wallace and my crew of pups. At Grandmae's, we wrote letters to Santa then decorated the envelopes with glitter and markers. After stuffing ourselves with Sett's homemade cinnamon buns, pulled from the freezer and warmed, we took a chilly walk to the mailbox to deliver the letters.

It wasn't enough. Nerves still prickled along the back of my neck. As soon as the festivities ended, the notes haunted me again. While the kids followed Wallace to cut down a Christmas tree from the back of the property, I collapsed into a plush chair. They bounded off, but I was stuck. Stuck in a vortex of theories and confusion and questions.

What connection did the deputy, Miss Raven, Judy, Crow, and I have? And why now? Did anyone else receive a delayed threat like Crow?

If Crow were here, he'd offer to help. With ice skating or step aerobics or another adventure. And he'd be right to recommend it.

Too frazzled to enjoy another cinnamon bun, I bid goodbye to Mae and wolfed out. I shifted to all fours and dashed from their rural property to Mockbuster. There, I shifted back, slipped into a fresh set of clothes, and splashed water onto my face. I resolved to take two hours to walk through the video shop and get ideas for my next play. If running couldn't get my brain to stop spinning, at least writing would redirect my focus and I could open my shop for a few hours.

The clock ticked one hour after another. Before I knew it, Wallace and Mae dropped the pups off to skate with friends at Roller Shakes while the new and tired grandparents got a bite to eat and finished holiday shopping.

I meandered through the rows of VHS tapes, but it only reminded me I'd made yet another promise. I was supposed to burn the tapes involved in Cliff's investigation. My gut clenched. Not only was every movie a special part of my collection, but the thought of more fire right now...

I couldn't do it. Not yet, not until I cleared my head.

Ten minutes later, I found myself in a chair at Everland Theater with a notebook and pencil. Maybe tonight I'd borrow Sett's BBQ and toss the tapes in there. Or throw them in the fireplace at Mae and Wallace's house. If I didn't destroy the tapes soon, would Cliff do the honors? Was he the connection between us all? He certainly hated reapers since they didn't successfully guide his spirit to the beyond when he'd died. That connected Miss Raven and Crow. He wasn't my biggest fan and apparently complained to Judy. But that wasn't grounds for arson, was it?

There simply weren't enough leads. I'd go in circles. *Just write, Noema.* I browsed my list of screenplay ideas, but none of them sparked a lightbulb. I flipped to a new page and scooted forward to prop my feet on the top of the seat in front of me. My black combat boots crossed over one another, exposing the Dr. Martens label on the soles. Worn red cushions sank beneath me, molding around my butt.

I blinked at the blank page.

After a murderer got involved in my last screenplay, I scrapped the project and shook off those memories, starting anew with a fresh idea.

Except no new ideas sprang forth. Nothing I was excited to write, anyway. I gave in, plucking the threatening notes from the front pocket of my hoodie. My sigh echoed against the curved ceiling designed to carry sound.

Weekday evenings left Everland Theater empty save for the humming ghost who was haunting the aisles in wait for her daughter to return. After I kept my promise to Bette, Hattie insisted Bette find Reed and bring him here for her to scrutinize. He may have a few good qualities, like financial competency and work ethic, but extra cash didn't impress Hattie. Her spirit fizzled with anxious energy as she paced across the stage in front of me.

"If you want more information about Zed and Reed, you could always ask Sett," I suggested. I tapped my pencil against my lips and watched as Hattie floated through the rows of chairs.

She froze and aligned the headpiece's golden ribbon with her hairline. The shiny pearl beads dangled just behind her left eye as she shook her head. "I'm not exactly his partner in fighting crime so I don't suppose he'll share details of an ongoing investigation."

She wasn't wrong. Sett was a stickler for rules. But he'd made an unspoken vow, deeming himself the guardian of Bewitcher's Beach like the gargoyles who used to watch over ancient cathedrals. If he thought giving Hattie more information would shield Bette from an unsavory relationship or a heart-aching breakup, he would.

"I can ask him, if that's what you're hinting at." I wasn't his partner against crime either. Nobody was. Sett worked alone at Bewitcher's Beach Police Department since the deputy left and Mayor Fitz stopped volunteering. Maybe Hattie believed the sheriff would share more with me since I'd helped solve a murder or two. Really, Sett preferred I didn't get involved.

"I never hint, Noema. You should know that." With every movement, her glittering gold dress cast dazzling spots of lights around the theater. "This is why I prefer the company of fairies. They cannot lie."

"You're the one lying right now. You barely tolerate Barney lately." Their on and off flirtation was more of an emotional rollercoaster than *Sleepless in Seattle*. "Plus, your best friend is a werewolf, so I beg to differ. You don't prefer fairies." I fluttered my eyes at her, knowing she was only on edge because of Reed. Surely, a lighthearted chat would lift her mood before she haunted the darn kid.

"Ah, so you're saying choosing you as my best friend was where I went wrong." She pointed at me. "Why don't you stop jabbering and leave me to my thoughts? I happen to know you haven't picked a new premise for a screenplay. You'll never keep your promise if you don't start writing it."

Another promise. Oops. Maybe I was better at thinking before I acted lately—but thinking before I spoke, before I swore to track a criminal or write a play or burn VHS tapes—was another story. I still had a long way to go.

Of course the promise Hattie referred to was an old one. One I'd made to my late husband.

A promise I'd made to follow my dreams. A twinge flickered in my chest. Though Christopher had long passed, and I'd buried the guilt I felt for turning him into a werewolf, the promise was still a fresh wound. After seven years, I'd yet to complete a single screenplay. I started dozens and finished even more stage plays for our local theater. But screenplays? Something to send to a Hollywood agent? I couldn't bring myself to complete any.

Hattie prattled on about fairies and telling the truth and how, even though Barney was a grump, at least he was bold enough to speak his mind. I fiddled with the threatening notes from my pocket, piecing the torn papers together. Against the white lined paper of my notebook, Crow's note appeared dirty, perhaps by our greasy fingers. Except the note from Mockbuster's door was a shade off-white too. I squinted, comparing the cream papers to the white notebook and then flipped them over, examining every corner. This shade of cream was awfully familiar. In the corner of the first note was a sliver of another color. I brought it close enough to my face that my nose poked the middle of the page.

Green? Dark green. Cream and green... My pulse thumped in uneven bursts as understanding dawned on me. These papers matched the colors of The Oyster Inn. And since Barney never lied, he'd admit why I'd received threats written on his stationery. That was, if he knew.

My black boots hit the floor with a heavy thud and I popped to my feet, alarming Hattie into a gasp.

"And they say *ghosts* are startling." She rolled her eyes at me. I waved the notes in the air, and as I hurried for the door, she followed. "What is it, Lassie? Timmy fell down the well again?"

It was my turn to roll my eyes. "I'm not in my wolf form, I can speak just fine thank you very much."

"That's not what I see." Her sapphire eyes raked over me, and her chin tilted. "Claws, fur, fangs..."

I looked down at my hands where my fingernails stretched into thick sharp claws and fur sprouted over my skin. I drew a slow breath, and evidence of the wolf receded. Was I more disturbed by the threats than I'd thought? First the slash attack on Crow's shirt, then the tension when Reed followed me to Mockbuster, and now this.

But it wasn't fear; the heady burn of smoke confirmed that. Rage roiled in my chest, and the mere thought of fire coming for my home made me want to howl a warning. I'd just built a true pack, friends that felt like family, and this mysterious yet cowardly note-writer was trying to take it all away.

"Well?" she prodded.

"I have a clue." I held up the notes. "Thanks to your rambling on about fairies and Barney, I finally figured out what these papers reminded me of." Hattie raised her brows, impatiently awaiting the answer of which I held her in suspense. "And considering it's probably stationery from The Oyster Inn, it's not looking good for Zed...and Reed."

Hattie's mouth fell open, and she shooed me away. "What on earth are you waiting for? Go. Get evidence for Bette that Reed is not worth her time."

That wasn't exactly my intention or goal, but I obliged, slipping out the doors. I crossed the narrow alley that separated the large theater from the quaint inn. Sunshine blazed low on the horizon and warmed my cheek on an otherwise frigid evening.

The yellow rays were disappearing, but it was a welcome brightness that put a skip in my step while it lasted. I stood on The Oyster Inn's doormat and held up the first note against the cream paneled walls. Closing one eye, I assessed whether my assumption was correct. The paper blended perfectly, and the sliver of forest green matched the paint on the window's flower boxes. The marigolds didn't bloom in winter, but the boxes were just as cheerful with bright red ribbons tied to each corner.

I twisted the knob and stepped inside where a thick Christmas tree with the same red ribbons stood at the left corner. The massive check-in desk was ornate wood, carved with little oysters in the design and painted cream to match the light and airy theme of the inn. The desk was empty with Barney nowhere to be seen. A crystal chandelier glittered overhead, and though the style was a bit too fancy compared to the ruffled curtains and quaint colors, the glitz perfectly represented the finery of Barney's establishment.

Raucous laughter drew my attention to the right where a pixie poured cocktails at a small bar. A few patrons who sat on the tall green vinyl stools chatted and sipped the mixed drinks. Mae and Wallace enjoyed one of their routine date nights with two glasses of blood red wine. The half-dragon leaned past her husband to clink her cup with Mayor Fitz's mug. Beside him sat Zed.

I found myself drifting toward them, trying to catch a bit of their shared conversation and the concoction of smells that surrounded them. There, mingled among the citrusy emotions of the cheerful gang, the bite of alcohol, and a hint of gardenia perfume wafting from Mae, was the distinct spicy sweet burn of nicotine. Or was it just from the blend of aromas with a sting of Cabernet Sauvignon?

"Noema!" Wallace spotted me and waved me closer. "Have a glass with us."

"Well hello there, Noema," Mayor Fitz, rosy-cheeked and a little tipsy, shouted with even more enthusiasm than usual. If that were possible for the ever-positive man. He stood to offer me his chair, but I waved for him to sit back down. "Mae tells us Crow is a target now too. Do you and Sett have any suspects yet?"

I shook my head as I tried my best not to glance at Zed. The nicotine. The Oyster Inn stationery. But he wasn't the only man who'd popped into my head when Mayor Fitz asked the question. Cliff haunted my thoughts. He was just so doggone bitter. If he took it upon himself to destroy anything he considered a tether...*Curses!* My part in this was overdue. It was past time I burned those tapes.

I fiddled with the notes in the pocket of my jean jacket. Because Cliff had no reason to use Oyster Inn stationery, my attention settled on the blonde man at the end.

Zed was guzzling a cheap beer from the can. He slammed the empty can down and then stood, exchanging a word with Mayor Fitz before he excused himself. With every step he took, my eyes tracked him until he vanished up the staircase.

Mayor Fitz noticed me watching and promptly filled me in on the deal. "Zed has offered to fix Judy's house pro-bono." The mayor's eyes sparkled as brightly as his hairless head. "But I bet he has a secret plan." My heart skipped, and I glanced back at the stairs. Fitz gave Judy a friendly nudge with his elbow, but the librarian only shot him an annoyed glare. "Once she sees the work he's done on my house, she'll want to remodel her whole cottage."

"With my approval!" Mae interjected.

"He just wants to leave a legacy. I know a thing or two

about that. That's why I encouraged Dr. Pitt to run for mayor. My leadership will leave a legacy through him next term."

"If he doesn't win *this* term."

The interruption didn't suck the wind out of Mayor Fitz's sails. "I'll tip the scales back in my favor after tomorrow night's speech. It's a doozy!"

I tuned out the rest of their conversation.

Was that Zed's plan? Torch the houses, then offer some pro-bono repair that convinced property owners to pay for more updates and remodels? It seemed like a lot of extra work, but I supposed desperation pushed people to do strange things.

With empty glasses now, the group dispersed and said their goodbyes. Mae and Wallace headed for the door while Mayor Fitz tipped the bartender.

I spun around to see Barney had returned to the check-in desk. In a beige cardigan and hunched over a newspaper, he pinched his glasses in one hand and shook the newspaper until the flopping edge stood upright. His cheeks sunk inward as if puckered by a sour lemon and his gaze roved over the inky news. Nobody would know Barney was a fairy with his wings always tucked in his endless wardrobe of brown cardigans and the occasional tweed coat. Though he never admitted it, I always wondered if he'd had an encounter with a hunter since he was one of the few people in Bewitcher's Beach who concealed his supernatural side.

I crept across the marble on the balls of my feet, stepping carefully so as to not irritate the man who often accused me of being too loud. He wasn't wrong. Despite tip-toeing, my bulky combat boots still thunked with every step. Now that the bar was empty, the only other sound was the quiet rhythmic swish of the pixie's rag wiping down the counter.

Barney blinked, and he peered at me through the thick wiry gray hair of his long eyebrows. The curling hairs matched the overgrowth in his nostrils. He yanked the glasses off and squinted down his nose. "Noema. Have my complaints finally made a difference?"

I frowned and folded my ears back.

"Bah. Wishful thinking on my behalf." He closed the newspaper and leaned both elbows on it, lacing his meaty fingers through one another. "Sett will never make you move. He's too smitten with you. But living in a building zoned only for commercial use is a blatant affront to the law!"

My skin prickled, though this complaint wasn't news. He'd harassed me for living in the loft above Mockbuster for months now. As a self-appointed member of the unofficial town council, he'd always followed policy. As much as he disturbed me, I couldn't blame him for the threats. Like Hattie said, Barney never lied and never hid his true thoughts. The grumpy fairy would never resort to cowardly notes, much less take matters into his own hands to shove me and the pups out of our home.

"Sett is not smitten—"

"Then why hasn't he kicked you out of there? He's too nice to you and those rowdy mess makers."

"Excuse me!" I interrupted, stomping my boot against the marble. "You will not call my children 'mess makers.'" Though it was true. "Or rowdy." Also true. "Those adjectives are reserved for their mother and only their mother. And that's enough about Sett—who is certainly not smitten with me. Since I'm dating Crow, I insist you speak no more of this nonsense and allow me to get to the matter at hand."

Barney's mouth dropped open, and his breath blew out a few scraggly mustache hairs. His eyes were wide and expectant. Maybe I was a little startling when I wanted to be, but it was Hattie who taught me how to be blunt and get to the point.

I cleared my throat and put the notes on the desk where the cream paper covered the headline of his newspaper. "Now, may I please see a pad of the stationery you provide for the guests?"

He squinted at the crumpled notes and grimaced. "Disorganized as always, I see." He spoke as he bustled around, shuffling to the other end of the long desk. "If you're going to scribble your screenplays on Oyster Inn stationery, I demand you don't crinkle the paper. Everything down to the complimentary stationery represents me and my inn." He grunted as he stooped to reach a low drawer. When he straightened, he huffed, breathless from the single squat. Even Miss Raven couldn't frighten Barney into a little exercise to extend his life. He rubbed an open palm over his bulging belly as he shuffled back, slapping the pad of paper on the desk. "I keep my inn pristine. Something of which a woman who frequently dons wrinkled shirts and worn-out jeans wouldn't understand."

Again, he wasn't wrong and he never lied, but a bit of tact would have been nice. I glanced down at my old Stevie Nicks t-shirt and the jean jacket I wore every time my hoodies were in the wash. Ignoring his slight, I picked up the stationery pad. As suspected, every matching page was marked with an Oyster Inn symbol. Each paper had a giant "O" designed to look like a stark white pearl sitting at the base of three stalks of green seaweed.

The notes had been cut to rid the paper of the symbol, but the sliver of evidence remained. Whoever threatened us used Oyster Inn stationery. The arsonist was likely one of Barney's customers, staying right next door to Everland Theater and Mockbuster where they could look out the windows and spy on me. With that view, they'd know exactly when I left so they could swoop in and torch it.

I scooped up the notes, revealing the headline of Barney's newspaper. *Governor Steel swears to stop crime in its tracks!* The picture of a suave man in a suit inspired the kind of confidence we needed in Bewitcher's Beach. Hopefully, like Governor Steel, Mayor Fitz could do the same before crime increased. In the meantime, I'd sniff out whoever used Oyster Inn's notepads to spread threats.

First, I had to rule out Cliff. Tonight, after I called Crow for support, Cliff's tether was toast.

CHAPTER 11
LIGHTEN UP

EXACTLY ONE HOUR LATER, Hattie, Crow, and I stood over a metal trash can behind Mockbuster. To an outsider, the three of us probably resembled troublemaking teenagers in a back alley. Crow held a fire extinguisher at the ready, I hugged *The Swan Princess* to my chest, and Hattie pursed her lips at me, impatient. The other tapes were already alight, melting and turning to ash in the shiny metal bin.

I'd yet to sacrifice the final tape. My favorite cartoon film. Relief rippled through me as Hattie shifted her attention to Crow, and I could cling to the movie a fraction longer.

Her gemstone eyes raked over him, a smirk at her perfectly ruby lips. "Awfully nice of you to come all the way back into Bewitcher's Beach for this illegal little project."

A single dark curl fell into his left eye and, after he shook his head to knock it away, he shrugged. "I'm all in for a good party."

My gaze switched between them. As long as they chatted, Hattie wasn't pressuring me to toss the tape into the fire. *The Swan Princess* had a precious memory attached to it. Popcorn and homemade cookies with Sett and the kids and a slew of cartoon movies.

"You call this a party? You need to get out more," she said. Smoke billowed in her face and heat radiated in front of her, making it look as though her ghostly figure was underwater. Flames licked at her glittering gold dress, causing no harm, no interaction at all.

"Yeah?" Crow grinned and cocked his head. "Then you'll have to show me a real party sometime. I bet a flapper girl knows all about illegal partying. Maybe a little bootlegging."

"A little?" She snorted. "Listen, Mac—"

"My name's Crow."

I elbowed him. "It's slang from the 1920s." Hattie went full flapper girl whenever a handsome man was around. But this was new. Apparently, she considered Crow rather *dapper*. Was it his affinity for parties? Either way, I wanted them to keep talking. I hugged the tape tighter, as if embracing it would bring back simpler times before the protection spell came down and murderers and arsonists arrived on Bewitcher's Beach's doorstep. Or, shore.

"As I was saying." Hattie shot us both a sharp glare. "If we get this broad away from the fuzz one of these days, I'll show you a party like you wouldn't believe."

Crow threw his head back and laughed. All that talk of illegal activity actually worked. I laughed too, relaxing enough to loosen my grip on the tape. Before Hattie could harass me to get it done and over with, I got it done and over with.

The Swan Princess fell into the metal can with a thud, and the flames poofed up. Sparks danced around, vanishing into tiny black specks as they floated to the concrete. The fire cracked, giving sound to how my heart felt as it devoured the tape. And destroyed Cliff's tether. At least something good came of this. Cliff's spirit would release, and we'd cross a suspect off the list.

Once the tape disintegrated into nothing but ashes, Crow sprayed the fire with the extinguisher and we dispersed. Hattie phased through Everland Theater's walls, and I walked Crow to his car parked at the front of the shop. We said goodbye, and he promised to call in case Hattie decided to throw a banger. Or if I needed anything.

I wrapped my arms around myself, alone now as the black Honda Accord sputtered away on the cobblestone. The cool air encouraged the tension crowding in my jaw and shoulders to melt away. On this side of Mockbuster, the smoke from our trash fire was only a hint of fumes in the ocean air.

I turned to the shop when a devious face manifested into existence. My pulse stuttered and I nearly swallowed my tongue. Cliff materialized between me and Mockbuster's door, appearing scratchy as though he was a television with a wonky antenna. *He was supposed to be gone with the tapes...*

The temperature dropped another few degrees from his towering, floating apparition. I frowned at his folded arms and rolled my eyes to meet his sneering gaze.

"When are you going to torch those tapes?" he asked.

My breath swirled through his chest and then disappeared. "I just did." And clearly it failed.

Silence. After a moment, he narrowed his eyes. "You lie."

"Never." I threw up my hands in surrender.

"You must have done it wrong. Those were the items I died touching. Did they completely burn to ashes? What about the cases the tapes were in?" The venom in his voice pitched higher and higher. Spittle flew from his mouth. "Do I have to do everything myself to make sure it's done right?" He fiddled with a shiny object in his hand, but with his fingers solidified enough to hold it, I couldn't see through his skin. The edge of the sleek metal surface caught the lamplight's glow. A distinct metallic sound clicked. Just like a lighter.

Cliff clenched it into a fist and smacked his knuckles against his other palm. The meaty thwack of the hit sent alarm bells ringing in my head until I determined the behavior was merely a habit of his impatience. Of course he could interact with his own body, but it still looked wrong—the sound of bone whacking against flesh when he had neither. Cliff had quickly learned how to solidify his apparition, which meant he could interact with other objects when he put the effort in. Objects like gasoline and lighters and cigarettes.

"Do you smoke?"

"Excuse me?" His jaw clenched, and evidence of the plastic surgery he'd had in life was apparent. His sharp jawline didn't match his soft, rounded features. Or perhaps his manifestation was buzzing with static again. "Do I look like I can smoke or eat or drink? Hell, I'd kill for a cold bottle of Budweiser." His eyes glazed over, and the momentum of his rage temporarily lulled.

I cleared my throat. "I meant when you were alive." Ghosts often tried to return to their old habits. Like how Hattie enjoyed the smell of her former favorite foods even if she couldn't bite into a deviled egg or a green olive.

"I was a doctor," he said as he hunched low, hunkering down to the level of my face. Though I ran hot as a werewolf, it was already too chilly tonight. His icy presence caused me to step back and avoid the ghostly freeze. "What do you think?"

A heavy footfall scraped against the cobblestone. "Is there a problem here?" Sett's deep voice shocked us from a staredown. Cliff won, since I blinked and took another step away from him. He curled his upper lip, becoming the perfect picture of a classic villain. Sett gently put his hand on my back and raked his eyes over me. "Everything okay, Noema?"

Moments like these reminded me of a nickname we'd once called each other. He was my backup when I got into trouble. I was his when he'd finally accepted my help on investigations. My skin tingled where he touched me, and a hint of guilty rotten fish emanated from me. If I squinted, I'd see the bright shine of Roller Shakes' milkshake statue in the distance behind Sett's head.

Would the way Sett was looking at me right now bother Crow? Of course not. I was merely another townsperson for Sett to watch over. That was all. The fishy stench dissolved, giving my nausea a relief.

"I'm okay," I assured him.

"Her?" Cliff spat. "You should be asking me. I'm the one who was murdered and then trapped here. Noema owes me for sticking her nose in my case. I think my spirit must have stuck to something at her poor excuse for a shop." As he spoke, Cliff ducked closer to me again, surging forward until his icy nose nearly gave mine frostbite. I shuddered and shuffled away, pushing against the pressure of Sett's hand. Sett dropped it and stepped around me and into Cliff's apparition. The ghost floated back, offended by the blatant disregard for his presence.

With Sett inserted between us now, the risk of frostbite melted. "That's enough." My pulse thudded as Sett's muscular wings expanded into a protective wall, blocking Cliff's view of me. If Sett backed up a mere inch, I'd be pressed against him.

"What are you going to do, arrest me?" Cliff chuckled.

"I know you're new to being a ghost, Mr. Conflick, so you may not know this, but I can just as easily take you in with a ghost trap as I can anyone else with handcuffs."

Cliff only scoffed and muttered under his breath as he spun and surged away. The apparition of the murdered man blinked from one location to the next as he made his way down the street and back toward the shore where he haunted the beach house. Despite the distance between me and the angry ghost, I couldn't release the pent up air in my lungs.

Sett tightened his wings, folding them into his body when he turned and gave me a once over. "Do you have time to grab a bite with me? My treat." His chin tilted and eyes flickered to Roller Shakes. *My treat.* Before I could spiral over the details of a potential date despite the fact that I was already dating Crow, Sett clarified. "I have some information."

My heart skipped. "So do I." I glimpsed through the glass and inside Mockbuster. The clock on the yellow wall read half-past midnight. "What are you doing over here so late anyway?"

"Checking on...Mockbuster."

Did he smell the smoke? Sense our illegal burning? Sett wasn't above arresting me. I needed to get him away from here before he noticed. I lifted my chin toward the massive milk-shake across town. Roller Shakes was the only spot in town still open. "How about we talk over a midnight snack? Hattie can keep an eye on my shop."

"Only if I'm buying."

I nodded, and he tucked his hands into his coat.

At Roller Shakes, Sett leaned forward, elbows on the table and attention fixed on me. Heat flushed my cheeks, and I couldn't help but glance at the door to Crow's office. But he wasn't there, and this was merely an exchange of information. Not a date. So why the heck was I blushing?

"The investigation has progressed," he began. I waited for him to continue, but impatience got the best of me when he stayed silent. Knowing Sett, he was dying to share valuable information but respected the rules of manners when it came to "ladies first."

"Was it Zed?" I blurted. Sett only tilted his head so I kept going. "I traced the notes back to The Oyster Inn stationery where he's been staying."

Before he could respond, a gorgeous vampire wheeled up on roller skates with a tray that carried our orders. Cordelia's long black hair billowed around her waist when she came to a stop and flashed us a dazzling fanged grin. Skillfully, she balanced the tray in one palm and doled out a plate with a burger, another with chicken strips, and two paper soda cups with blue zig zags across the center. I chugged the Diet Pepsi, and as soon as the syrupy soda fizzed on my tongue, all thoughts of Cliff, threatening notes, and fires didn't seem so bad. At least for now.

Sett took a quick bite of the juicy burger, the crisp lettuce crunching under his teeth. He swallowed and leveled with me. He didn't answer my inquiry, posing a question of his own instead. "You're sure the notes are from the inn?"

I nodded, taking another sip of soda. "Yep. Both papers match Barney's stationery."

"Well, it wasn't Zed. He has an alibi." This time, I bit my tongue and let him talk. "He and Reed were seen on a security camera shopping at Chanel's boutique for Zed's wife during the time of the first fire." That explained why they were walking near the studio. I scraped my memory. Reed dropped by class to visit with Bette, but he wasn't there long. He likely met up with his dad when he left. "Noema..." He set the burger down and took a long breath. "I really think you should go on that road trip. Get out of here for a few days—"

"No." I shook my head and swiped the paper cup for another swig of liquid courage. "I can't leave Mockbuster exposed. It's my entire life, Sett. I know the deputy left and his place was spared, but we don't know this creep will stay consistent. They're a criminal, which means they're probably a liar too. Aerobics Alive was attacked with all of us inside, which is different from what happened to Judy's cottage. No pattern.

Judy's was torched with nobody home. I keep picturing the same happening to Mockbuster."

"Noema."

"And the kids are safe and happy with Mae and Wallace until we catch this guy." *Or ghost.* If it wasn't Zed, Cliff's threats and sudden intimidating appearances and complaints felt more serious. And now he believed my attempt at tape torching—or tether destruction—was done incorrectly. "I can't bear to separate them during the holidays."

"I know you well enough to know I can't convince *you* to stay at Mae's too."

"I can't risk losing my business and my home. My kids' drawings will be gone. All those classic movies would take forever to replace. If I run away, they'll have an unwatched building to light up to their heart's content."

He sighed. "There's something else. Between my investigation and the fire marshal's, we've determined it's likely the fire at Aerobics Alive was set from the inside."

"What? Who's your suspect?" My mind swirled with possibilities, considering the faces of the students who took step aerobics. I didn't believe any of them would be willing to start a fire. When he opened his mouth, I cut him off. "What about someone who could manifest inside the back of the studio without any of us noticing? Cliff could have started the fire and then blinked away just like we saw him move down the street."

Sett nodded. "I'll be questioning him again, but I don't have anything solid to bring him in. There'll be another round of routine questioning for everyone who was in class that day."

"Okay, shoot. Let's get this out of the way," I said, hinting for him to get on with the questioning. Because even though Sett knew it wasn't me, he followed policy every step of the way. It was likely the reason he'd requested this meeting.

When he shook his head, my face went cold, blood draining away.

"Thank you, but no. I'm here to tell you to be careful, Noema. The problem is, I have no solid leads, and this situation is getting scarier by the day. It could be Cliff just as well as it could be any of the dozens of people in that class. The motivation is as unclear as the suspect list." Silence hung between us as his slate eyes fixed, unblinking. His jaw was set, and it was then I noticed the chink in his steadfast armor, the crack in the calm he claimed as appointed guardian of Bewitcher's Beach. He was worried he'd fail to shield me—one of the Bewitched citizens he swore to serve. "You really should leave."

I bristled.

Nobody could tell me to run away with my tail between my legs and leave behind everything I fought to build. The home I created for me and the pups after Christopher passed. The shop. The stepping stone to my dream of working and writing the movies I so desperately loved. And definitely not after I made a promise to Judy I'd find the person who dared threaten us.

CHAPTER 12
BLOWING SMOKE

FOR MOST OF the next day, I was busy behind the register at Mockbuster. Irregular hours made it difficult for movie buffs to get their fix, so I forced myself to slow down and work. I still had to keep the lights on and food on our table when this was all over. And if I did lose my business to a criminal, it was all the more reason to make a few extra bucks now. Plus, I kept my ears perked for traveling news, gossip, and rumors spread by customers.

After the sun hit the horizon, customers dwindled, and I flicked off the light of the open sign. I rushed next door to retrieve the kids and prepared for a merry evening of brand new holiday traditions.

In Christmas sweaters and with mugs of hot cocoa in hand, we met up with Mae and Wallace for caroling before the tree lighting ceremony.

Our singing was off-key and the night was cold, but the bright lights and warm energy lifted my spirits. We finished an off-rhythm rendition of "Frosty the Snowman" and then headed to the park.

A massive pine tree had been hauled in from the forest

behind Roller Shakes. Broad poles and ropes staked it to the ground to resist wind. Hundreds of thousands of lights draped over every branch, ready but not yet illuminated. Tonight, Mayor Fitz would do the honors of plugging in the cord. Everyone was eager for the cheerful sight amidst the chaos created by the arsonist. Especially me.

Bewitched citizens young and old and every person in between huddled together, chatting, gossiping, swapping holiday stories. I listened, trying to recall everyone at Aerobics Alive on the day of the fire. Mentally, I retraced each person's steps as far as I could remember, but it got trickier to place everybody as I went along. I hadn't been paying attention that day, too busy trying to avoid embarrassing myself.

Mayor Fitz took to the stage, the area currently dark except for the glow of lamp posts. "Welcome Bewitched friends!" He boomed into the microphone then lifted it to wave to the crowd. Cheers rippled. "Thanks to this morning's release of *The Bewitcher's Beach Gazette*, we all know updates on the current investigation." A slip in his voice piqued my ears. For once, Mayor Fitz didn't sound like a perfectly cheerful big red bow. But the uncertainty vanished as quickly as it came. "So I'll only say one thing on the matter before we zip along to happier news. If I'm reelected, I'll bring new support to Bewitcher's Beach. Seers, spellcasters, firefighters, and police!"

Though more security was an attractive promise, all we really needed was the original spell that sheltered the town and for the deputy to return. Did Mayor Fitz already consider Judy a lost cause and planned to replace her with another spellcaster?

His speech moved on. With the microphone returned to the stand, he lifted the power cord above his head, ready to plug the tree in.

The tree illuminated, and the kids went wild. Stevie shrieked and pointed. "Grandmae, look!"

Thousands of brilliant colorful bulbs glistened like magic hovering over the pine needles. The display was nothing more than simple strings of light, but alight and with family by our side, it was an enchantment all its own.

Babette released a screeching yip, disintegrating the moment of perfection. I snapped my attention to the little dog at Mae's ankles. Babette bared her tiny canines and barked, then spun around to furiously scratch at Mae's legs. A shadow cast over the dog, blocking the light of the lamp post nearby. I looked up to see Sett had elbowed his way through the crowd, his hand on Mae's arm. The sheriff avoided eye contact with me as he quietly spoke to Mae. A minute passed before she nodded and shifted Babette's leash to Wallace. Babette went wild, yipping and growling at Sett.

Was this the start of the routine interviews? No matter how tall I stretched my ears, I couldn't catch a word they said through the chatter.

Mae flashed me a look. Her mouth twisted, and she clutched tightly to her knitted bag. Wrinkles bunched at her forehead, and the pungent odor of ammonia sloughed off of her with a hint of burnt toast. What did Sett say that made her afraid and regretful? Another smell mixed in, possibly from Wallace. The rainy aroma matched Wallace's downcast expression as the sheriff guided Mae on a weaving path through her neighbors and friends.

I wedged past Cordelia and Chanel to reach Mae. "Is everything okay?"

Mae's throat rippled with a hard swallow, and she released a forceful breath. "I don't know if I'll be able to watch the kids tonight. I'm sorry, Noema. Sett's taking me to the station."

"What?" I shot Sett a scowl and lowered my voice so

nobody could catch my words. "You can't seriously suspect Mae?"

"Noema." His voice was entirely too calm. Ugh. He was always too calm. Where was his fire for catching the real criminal? The same fire that raged in my ribcage at the smell of Mae's apprehension. I folded my arms and waited, relishing the icy breeze as it cooled me down faster than stretching. He sighed and addressed Mae, requesting that she make her way to the station ahead of him. When she obliged, he leaned in, aware of the likelihood of a dozen eavesdroppers. "I received a tip that she just switched insurance providers and raised her plan on both of these buildings."

My mouth dropped open. The tipper was a liar. "What about Mockbuster? She's not *my* landlord. Who the heck said this?"

"It was an anonymous call. I'm just going with the information I have right now. I'm not arresting her, but I need to go beyond the routine questions."

I growled but didn't have a retort. The tip was dead wrong. "Look, I know you have to follow protocol, but how dare you?"

"It's not personal."

"Ha! Isn't that what you said when you arrested me?"

"That wasn't personal either. You broke the law."

I huffed. Sure, I'd forgiven him for that already, but could I forgive him for this? "You're wasting your time—"

"You're right."

I clamped my jaw shut. I was right? *Curses.* That was the last thing I expected Sett to say. Now I struggled to form words around my dry tongue. I was allowing my impatience and temper to get the best of me and, before body odor choked me, I looked away. Thank heavens he couldn't smell the aftermath of my outburst. Embarrassment's icky stench would only double down on the humiliation.

Awkward silence dangled between us until he broke it. "It's not her. But maybe I can shake another clue out from any information she might have *while* following protocol." It wasn't the worst plan, but I hated the thought of Mae in that stuffy, cramped interrogation room. Sett reached out and gave my arm a quick squeeze before turning away.

I couldn't decide if the gesture comforted or infuriated me. I rubbed at the spot he touched and moved back. Thoughts spun as I shuffled back to the kids and Wallace.

Why would this anonymous tipper wait until now to try to pin the fires on Mae? What changed? My ears folded back as the answer came in a flash, the same way Cliff blinked into existence as he moved from one place to the next.

What changed was that Sett had informed Cliff he was capable of arresting ghosts.

LATER THAT NIGHT, the bedtime routine went smoothly and swiftly. Stevie picked a short book, *The Very Hungry Caterpillar,* from when they were wee pups.

Hattie came to my rescue, offering to have a sleepover for the pups in Everland Theater before I even had to ask. Wallace was home, but with his wife taken in for questioning late into the night, I didn't dare add four rowdy children to his stressful evening. While Hattie watched over them, I'd watch Bewitcher's Beach in case Cliff decided to strike.

Once the kids fell asleep, I tiptoed through the maze of sleeping bags that lined the floor of the front row. Halen and Dio softly snored while Jovi tossed and turned. The only one still awake was Stevie, who whispered to Squeaks and Sir

Crabby, both of whom perched on her pillow, listening intently to whatever far-fetched tale she told them.

I stooped to plant a kiss on Stevie's forehead and offer a quick pet to Squeaks. Sir Crabby wasn't friendly to anyone except Stevie and Squeaks, so I passed on the possibility of getting pinched and made my way up the theater and past the rows of worn seats. A green exit sign no longer lit up, but the dim lights beneath the steps still illuminated the dark aisles enough for me to see the steps leading to the doors. Hattie floated beside me.

"Thank you for watching them," I said.

Hattie lowered her chin in acknowledgment, her shimmery golden hair sweeping forward. "I know you're still worried about fire spreading from the shop into here, but I'll keep a keen eye on the theater while you watch Mockbuster." I nodded and swallowed through the squeeze in my throat. The thought of Mockbuster burning was bad enough, but adding destruction to Everland nearly drove me to tears. "Are you sure you want to stake out all night? You look wrecked."

I frowned and swiped my palm over my face, releasing a breath of exhaustion. "Gee thanks."

Hattie swirled her thin fingers around. "What? I'm a ghost, I don't need to sleep. But your plan to stay up all night like a guard dog in front of Mockbuster is going to age you faster than all that soda you drink."

I gave her a deadpan glare but couldn't argue with the truth. I was relying on nothing but hope and an adrenaline-fueled dream—plus my werewolf energy. And each of those were about as shredded as Crow's workout T-shirt. "I have to. Cliff acted like he was going to destroy everything until his spirit was released. So I'll be on the lookout at Mockbuster and watch town for smoke or suspicious activity. With Mae as Sett's focus now, the arsonist will be free to go wild."

"And you're sure Cliff's the arsonist?" Her thin, drawn brows knitted, pushing up the golden headband.

"I'm not sure, but I have to get Mae off Sett's suspect list. Plus, she was targeted only after she released the newspaper article about Aerobics Alive's fire coming from the inside. Cliff may have realized he could pin it on her and then continue torching whatever he believes is his tether."

"Mmm," she hummed. "It's a nasty business to be tethered for eternity. I've heard of it happening to other spirits. It's usually due to an unfinished business that they can no longer complete. Like apologizing to a loved one but the loved one passed on, so the spirit tethers to the loved one's wedding ring."

"Cliff knows this. Miss Raven said she told him all the possible tethers she knows of. But he's convinced it has to do with his murder investigation."

"He could try to get someone to slash him with a ghost blade if he wants to pass on," she said matter-of-factly, as if cutting a spirit with a magical blade was a mere daily task. I supposed a ghost who'd existed between life and death for seven decades wasn't afraid of the afterlife.

"I thought ghost blades were black market-level expensive."

She hummed again, spreading a haunting sound only a phantom could make. "They sure are. Seeing as they're made from black pearls, they cost a lot of sugar *and* they're painful to use. Plus, they're way too heavy for a ghost to lift, so someone else has to help, and good luck convincing a friend to stab you." A shudder rippled through her, sending the glittering fringe dress in a wave of gold. "But they're powerful buggers, imbued with magic to strengthen whoever wields it and sharp enough to cut through a mountain. The blade itself can act as a ghost trap if the spirit isn't ready to pass on. That's why no ghost would choose it unless they're as desperate and gutsy as this fellow sounds. It also leaves behind a scar in this world, and most of us don't want to be remembered with a scar."

"A scar?"

"When a spirit is knocked-off with a ghost blade, the ghost leaves behind a sort of screeching sound. It's annoying at best and embarrassing at worst. Not exactly the legacy I want people to know me by. But this punk obviously doesn't care about his reputation, so who knows."

"I'll give Miss Raven a call and ask if she suggested it to him. The sooner I figure this out, the sooner I get Sett's eyes off Mae. I already called him and tried to get him to question Cliff, but he said he had to finish interviews with everyone at Aerobics Alive first." I shook my head and scoffed. "Insurance scam. What a ridiculous idea." My hands curled into fists, ready to punch the man I suspected gave Sett the anonymous tip. Punching Cliff would hurt me more than it'd hurt him, risk of frostbite and all. Or knowing my clumsy butt, I'd swing so hard into thin air that I'd dislocate a shoulder. Forget doing step aerobics or wolfing out with a limb hanging out of its socket.

I walked next door to Mockbuster, fists still clenched and fingernails digging indents into my palms that matched the crescent moon suspended in the night sky. The shop was quiet, serene, and smelled of popcorn. After ringing Miss Raven, I meandered through the aisles of VHS tapes, running my finger over the tops of movie cases. Miss Raven assured me she'd already informed Cliff, but he rejected the ghost blade idea and he insisted he was right. If we burned all his possible tethers, he'd be free. Of course, Cliff wanted to be right.

I called and relayed this to Sett.

"I'll talk with Cliff as soon as I complete interviews with the studio's students," he said, his voice strained. Or tired. About as heavy as the sound of his footsteps.

I tried to keep the frown out of my own voice. "Will Mae be stuck at the station in the meantime?"

A sigh blew into the receiver like a gust of wind. "I sent her home with instructions to stay put."

That was better than nothing. But poor Grandmae didn't deserve to be under house arrest for the holidays.

"Slow as always," I muttered after bidding Sett goodbye and hanging up the phone.

What would my favorite heroines do if they were threatened by a man like Cliff?

Ripley from *Alien* would face the problem head on, likely wielding the ghost blade with no qualms about taking down the monster that threatened her. I shuffled from the science fiction section to the row of action movies. My gaze fluttered from the films to the view through the windows. The glass walls that lined the front of the store provided a full view of the sidewalk and the park beyond.

Thankfully nobody was lurking outside with a lighter and canister of gasoline. Not yet, anyway. That *nobody* without a body could show up any time. My patience wore thin, like lingering frustration while awaiting an unwound VHS tape to rewind. A shiver shuddered through me, and I returned to the comfort of my movies.

Ellie from *Jurassic Park* would do whatever it took to guard the children in her care. Even if it meant hiding and fleeing. The thought of kids had me absentmindedly drifting to the display of family films where I eyed the cover of *Little Women*.

"What would Jo March do?" My voice echoed in the silent space. Hair raised on the back of my neck. But speaking aloud might alert the arsonist I was here and that I could catch him in the act. I lifted my chin and whispered, "Jo would go for justice."

Bolstered now, I abandoned the aisles and readied to

hunker down at the front desk all night. Staying awake would at least give me time to pore over my list of screenplay ideas. *Which one will spark?* I winced. Bad choice of words.

The hard stool I sat on made me ache after the third hour, and I'd yet to like any of the ideas scribbled in my notebook. I stood to stretch my back and wander the store again, but a yawn split my mouth and my eyes drooped with the lull of sleep. Maybe Hattie was right. It was a fool's errand to try staying awake for so long.

Despite popular belief, even we energetic werewolves needed a little shut eye.

Still, I couldn't bring myself to go upstairs or let myself doze, so I wandered again, this time to the front door where a blast of fresh air might wake me. I yanked the door open, the bell chiming and startling a yelp out of me. I shook my head, silently chiding myself for the jumpy behavior. Outside, I closed my eyes and gulped chilly fresh air. The breeze soaked me with the scent of salt and damp sand until another smell arose, stinging my nose.

"Smoke," I whispered. My eyes shot open and I scanned Everland Theater and The Oyster Inn, then swept my gaze to the park and the buildings across town. In the distance, a puff of what looked like low-hanging clouds hovered over the office building that sat kitty corner from Mockbuster. Except the cloud was billowing. And black.

My throat constricted before I could release an alarming howl. The office building housed several businesses, but most notably wedged between it and the doctor's clinic, was the police station. Right where the cloud of smoke lingered.

Did Sett finally accuse Cliff and did Cliff retaliate? I didn't pause to think too long, instead scrambling inside to dial the emergency line. I rang the fire station first and then the police station, but Sett didn't answer.

My heart slammed into my stomach while the rest of my body shifted into my swiftest and fiercest form. As a werewolf, I bolted twice as fast from Mockbuster to the police station, loping and whimpering as I ran.

Maybe we weren't dating and maybe he made my blood boil, but I still felt like Sett's backup. I still felt enraged that he dared blame Mae, and yet I still prayed with every ounce of hope and energy and desperation that he was okay.

If Cliff *did* hurt Sett Lawrence, maybe I'd want to wield a ghost blade after all.

CHAPTER 13
A SPARK BETWEEN

I SKIDDED TO A HALT, claws scraping and scratching the cobblestone alleyway that branched between the police station and the clinic.

No flames in sight.

Tears welled behind my eyelids, but relief didn't belong. Not yet. A fire still raged somewhere, and Sett was missing in action.

I spotted the door of the police station left wide open and loped toward it, pausing at the threshold to release a howl. Nobody responded, which meant the station was empty. I barked again to be sure, but Sett wasn't here.

Had he responded to the fire? I took off, dodging behind the police station to find the source of the smoke. The row of cottages where Crow lived came into view. Smoke billowed above the house next to Crow's—the fire marshal's home. I whipped my head around, looking for her familiar face near the red truck parked in the alley. Another firefighter dragged a thick rubber hose to a fire hydrant, but his boss was nowhere to be seen. The fire marshal was missing, along with Sett.

Before my mind ran wild, the fire marshal stumbled out the

front door, coughing and sputtering. Fire ate away at the front porch, devouring the wood panels like kindling. The porch splintered and cracked, threatening to collapse beneath her. She jumped off the wood and into the grass before it buckled inward. A broad-shouldered figure appeared in the doorway, obscured by smoke.

Sett... The flames were blocking him now, making it impossible for him to exit the same way the fire marshal did. It was just like him as the appointed guardian of the town to barrel in and guide her out. Even to his own detriment.

Panic strangled my heart, which ramped with palpitations. A whimper escaped me, and I pawed at the ground, my claws grinding against stone. *Stone skin cracks too.* Though he was a gargoyle, muscular and forever calm, he was as vulnerable as anyone else.

He'd burn alive in there.

Sickness swirled in my gut. The fire marshal was struggling to breathe and the other firefighter was already engaged, battling the flames that licked and reached long orange fingers to the sky. It was up to me to help Sett find his way through the smoke. My front paws danced around until impatience overcame me.

I bolted for the back of the cottage, searching for one of the animal doors. Surely these older homes had a Creature Cutout for me to wedge through. I sniffed and scanned, but time was running out. Hopping up to a window, I placed my paws on the glass. Smoke clogged the whole of the house, but flames had yet to spread back here.

I clawed at the glass, barking. If he could hear me, maybe he could use my voice to track his way to the window and climb through. What if he was choking? If he made it to the back of the house, would he fit through the window? The questions were a blade digging deeper into my chest until I couldn't breathe. The smoke didn't help.

I barked and barked and barked until the shape of pointed wings emerged from the haze of the smoke on the other side of the glass.

Smoke and emotions strangled me like a leash wound too tightly. I pawed at the latch I couldn't reach from the outside. He was already on it, unhooking it and sliding the window open with a whack. I hopped down and backed up. Sett shoved it open then hefted himself up and over, landing in a cloud of dust that sparked a wracking cough.

The fire seemed to move at the speed of light as it followed Sett to the back of the house. Flames crackled, licking at the shingles and gutter above.

Another whine escaped me, but it was Sett who barked this time. "Noema! Back up!" I scrambled away from him before a wooden plank from the roof cracked and tumbled down.

I yelped and dodged away from the scorched board, nearly tripping over my own tail as I stumbled back. Another crack of splitting wood echoed from above, and the gargoyle moved faster than I'd ever seen before, feet slamming against the ground as he barreled toward me.

His stony shoulder smacked into my neck as he scooped me into his arms. He carried me out of the way before a second plank clattered to the cobblestone, flames eating away at the wood. My neck throbbed where he'd crashed into me. Gently, he returned me to all fours at a safe distance from fire and falling planks of wood.

Another wave of relief flooded me along with a jolt of heat. Nerves blazed through my veins as I tilted my snout to the sky and pinned Sett with my gaze.

I found myself examining his body for injury. My eyes raked

over his thick forearms, left bare where he'd pushed the sleeves of his police coat to his elbows, then found his massive wings, encircling his back like a protective blanket of muscle. Wrinkles around his eyes revealed that he smiled occasionally—when he wasn't surveying the city with his usual hardened stare. Nothing appeared wounded, but he could have inhaled too much fumes.

I skipped on my front paws and threw my head back, knowing he'd understand my agitation.

"I'm okay," he said. "Thank you." I snuffled and whined with a scratch at my snout. He released a breath with a sudden cough. When it subsided, he continued, knowing I was eager for answers now that we were all safe. "I was the first on the scene since I was staying late at the station. When I heard a noise back here, I tried to catch whoever started the fire, but they were gone once I made it to the back. All they left behind was this lighter. I thought the fire marshal was on duty tonight, but then I heard her shouting for help from inside before the truck arrived. So I ran in and helped her move rubble that had her trapped inside the bedroom." He lifted a shiny silver cylinder from the pocket inside his coat, careful only to touch the top and bottom rims. "Hopefully we can pull prints from this."

Another bark bubbled out of me as he descended into a second round of coughing. I shook my head once he cleared his throat and could focus on me. Sett tucked the evidence away and spoke again. "I know what you're saying. You think Cliff is to blame, and as a ghost, he left no fingerprints."

I barked, tail wagging for confirmation.

"Noema, I hate to say this, but I followed up on the claim from the anonymous tip and they were right. Mae recently changed her insurance, and the marshal's house is another building she owns."

I growled and scraped my claws against the stone sidewalk.

Someone was framing my friend, and I wouldn't let it happen without baring my fangs for a fight. Not a real fight, unless they decided to finally attack me and make good on the note's threat.

His wings twitched, expanding and then contracting ever so slightly like an alternative sigh. "I must go where the facts lead, and I'm sure they will lead me away from Mae. First, I have to follow the trail to figure that out."

I couldn't help the next growl that rumbled deep in my chest. *Ghosts don't sleep.* Cliff had to be the culprit. It simply made the most sense. As a first responder, the fire marshal was one of the many faces at the crowd on scene at Cliff's death. But she wasn't needed considering he'd already passed away when she got there. Did he blame her for not arriving soon enough? Did he consider something of hers a tether?

The fire hose rained down on the little cottage, extinguishing the flames once and for all. Though the time to rescue it was long past. The threat was tempered, but the damage was done, leaving this house far more destroyed than the burnt corner of Judy's cottage or the missing wall at Aerobics Alive. The arsonist was improving at getting the fire to spread faster. Or maybe the fire station and Sett were just slower, too overworked and overtired.

Lack of sleep forced another yawn out of me. It was probably well past two in the morning. All at once, bone-deep exhaustion tugged at every limb, and I longed to collapse on a pillow and curl up with my quilt. But Cliff was targeting everyone involved in his murder investigation, which meant I didn't have a second to rest. Sett and I would be next.

Side-by-side, Sett and I watched as the fire dwindled to soaked cinders. It left behind charred walls and a lingering sting of smoke. Even with the briny breeze sweeping through town, the fumes didn't clear out quickly enough.

Finally, he crouched and laid a hand on my back where the

fur was rough and knotted after tonight's run. "I don't think Cliff would be stupid enough to keep gasoline or anything suspicious at the house he haunts. But if he has nothing to hide, he might consent to a property search."

It was something, at least. I knew he had more probable cause to get a warrant and search Mae's house, but neither of us believed her guilty. Whoever had framed her and posted the anonymous tip was tricky, slippery. Smooth. Unlike Cliff's apparition that fuzzed and blinked like static electricity in a storm.

"I'm going to put as much time into investigating him as I can. I'll pay him a visit first thing tomorrow."

I nudged Sett's arm with my snout and barked my gratitude for sweeping me away from danger. Sett tilted his chin in appreciation and the barest smile comforted me, though a mix of emotions filled his eyes. My gut protested because, deep down, I knew my anger was unfair when he was simply following leads. It was his job. I shivered. How icky must it feel to have to investigate friends?

THE NEXT MORNING after a fitful sleep slouched in a chair at Everland Theater, I woke to the pups dancing around on the stage. Hattie swapped posts with me. I stayed with the kids, including Bette, who was forbidden from seeing Reed, while Hattie watched over Mockbuster until sunrise.

The few hours of tossing and turning yielded nothing but worry. Worry for the fire marshal, who'd received a threatening note around the same time as Crow, according to Sett. And worry for my home next. Why hadn't the arsonist struck Mockbuster yet? My note was one of the first. Was staying here keeping it safe? Unfortunately, that didn't match with what happened to the fire marshal. Though if Sett thought she was supposed to be on duty that night, maybe the arsonist did too.

Questions nagged me as I trudged through a fuzzy morning with a can of Diet Pepsi in hand. With Christmas almost here, our morning routine took much longer. Today was the last day of school, and each pup was rowdy and full of ideas for their holiday vacation. Halen announced his plan to create a home video based on the Power Rangers with his three siblings dressed as canine-style superheroes. Dio insisted we—including me—should spend the entire school break running soccer drills to get the most practice. Jovi quietly raised his book in the air as a signal that he'd be partaking in as much reading as possible. Stevie merely shrugged and mumbled something about visiting the forest on the outskirts of Bewitcher's Beach, likely to speak with woodland creatures for the sheer joy of befriending foxes and squirrels.

I dragged my tired butt to the Astro Van and drove them to their last class with a promise. "We'll reserve a day for each of you. That way we can do what everyone wants."

And if Sett and I pin the crimes on Cliff before then, we'll finally get to take a road trip to Shadowvale with Mae and Wallace along for the adventure. As much as I liked celebrating Christmas in town, I longed for answers. The search for our extended family through the *Book of Prophecies* called to me like a dream sequence in a movie scene. But that dream was on a distant horizon now and hours away at Shadowvale.

After a tornado of hugs, kisses, searching for backpacks, pulling jackets on, and stuffing the last bits of Eggo waffles in their mouths, the van was quiet again. I watched until the kids disappeared inside the maze of colorful buildings at Bewitcher's Beach Elementary with dozens of other shapeshifters, humans, gargoyles, fairies, sirens, half-dragons, and trolls. I shifted the van into drive and eased forward in the dropoff line until I was on the main street in town. It was only a minute's drive to the beach house Cliff haunted.

If Cliff felt cornered, Sett might need my help. Backup help.

I passed the library and the park where volunteers for Mayor Fitz's campaign set up for tonight's speech. Once I turned onto Beach Street, Cliff's massive house came into view. As suspected, Sett's police vehicle was parked in front of the picket fence surrounding the property. The two-story beach-front home had a matching white wraparound porch and seagull statues perched at the top of the staircase that reminded me of guard dogs. Though Cliff didn't need anything guarding it. He haunted the place well enough on his own, keeping people away.

Sett stood on the wide wraparound porch conversing with the ghost, whose manifestation scratched and blinked. Either Cliff had not consented to a search or the sheriff had only just arrived.

Quietly, I slipped from the driver's seat and closed the van's door. Sett didn't look in danger, and I wouldn't be able to smell Cliff's emotions, but I wanted to hear what Cliff had to say for himself. He'd threatened me more than once now, and it was only fair that I stood up for myself, showing him I wouldn't tuck tail and run.

"I don't even know who Judy is," he said to Sett as I climbed the porch steps.

"The librarian," Sett said. "Where were you between the hours of one and one thirty this morning?"

Come on, Sett. He won't confess that. Ask the real *questions.*

"Is that a ghost joke? Because I don't sleep?" Cliff wagged his wispy finger in Sett's face.

"Not in the slightest. I've been made aware of your

increasing threats regarding your murder investigation, and the same group of people has been targeted by an arsonist. It is in my best interest to know your whereabouts during each of these destructive events."

Cliff laughed. The raspy sound revealed he'd smoked more than a few cigarettes while he was alive, which didn't match his claim. *I'm a doctor, what do you think?*

I wrinkled my nose and frowned, sidling up behind Sett. Cliff's attention snapped to me, and my blood chilled. "You called your dog to come attack me, huh, sheriff?"

"I'm not a dog."

"Noema." Sett greeted me with a faint nod, but his eyes said more. *What are you doing here?* The same thing I was doing last night, watching his back in case the ghost got angrier.

"For *your* information," Cliff continued, pointedly staring at Sett and only Sett, "I was here, haunting this creaky house and bored to death." His eyes slid to me. "Hell, if I could get out of Bewitcher's Beach and see the world, maybe I wouldn't be losing my mind."

I grimaced. "What about when Judy's house was attacked? What were you doing?"

"I still have no clue who this Judy is and, frankly, I don't care."

"The fire, at the cottage between Beach Street and CC Court," Sett clarified. "That is Judy Knovel's house."

Cliff blew a raspberry through pursed lips and then chuckled. "Look, you're both grasping at straws, clearly desperate to pin some crimes on an easy scapegoat, the guy who doesn't even want to be here. I'm not part of the Bewitcher's Beach *family*." His voice dripped with sarcasm. "Which also means I don't care enough about you people or this place to spend my time starting irrelevant fires. I just want to get out, and like I said, I don't even know Judy other than talking to her once or twice at the library."

I chewed my bottom lip, my shoulders tense as I folded my arms tightly around my torso. They weren't irrelevant fires. Not with so many of us having been involved in his investigation. If only I could smell a ghost's emotions, I'd know if he was lying.

Sett scribbled on his notepad. The pencil scratching dry paper and the calm crash of waves were the only sounds breaking the tense silence. Finally, he flipped his notepad closed and nodded at the beach house. "Will you allow me to take a quick look around?"

"I don't see the point," Cliff leveled with Sett, folding his arms. With a quick glance at me, he added, "You're barking up the wrong tree. These are all buildings owned by Mae Wild-fyre right? The same smoky broad who sold me this dump." He gestured at the beautiful beach house. How he could call it a dump, I couldn't fathom. "Doesn't she basically breathe fire? I'll bet it's her pinning this on me."

I couldn't stop the little gasp that popped out, and both men looked at me. I avoided Sett's knowing gaze. *Curses.* We had nothing on Cliff, which meant Mae was still the lead suspect.

"What?" Cliff shrugged. "She's not my biggest fan after I insulted this house. She doesn't want me haunting this place, but it's nicer than the rest of this cesspool. So until I get away from this town, I'm not moving out of this house. Oh, and did you know she was a bank robber in her younger years?" A smug grin curled half his mouth.

In fact, we *did* know. Mae was long retired from her life of crime and had paid her dues since then. Cliff's behavior was far more suspicious. A memory itched at the back of my brain.

"Wait!" I thrust a finger in the air. "What about that lighter you carry around? Where's that?"

He was solid enough to fiddle with an object in his hand. When he opened his fist to reveal it, the pale glow of his apparition glinted off the steel. If he had the lighter in his possession, it couldn't be the same one Sett found outside the fire marshal's house. *Doggone curses.* "This thing? It was engraved by my first wife for when I occasionally indulged in a fine cigar." An odd and unexpected faraway gleam flickered in his eyes as his gaze fell to his palm. "It's the last object I have that's worth more than half this house." His fingers folded over it. "Couldn't have a Bewitched stealing it for its value." Venom clipped his voice, and he stared at me before narrowing his eyes at Sett. "Look, if helping you bumpkins find the arsonist will get you to focus on *my* tether sooner, then allow me to offer a hand."

With that, Cliff disappeared and manifested again on the porch steps. He blinked across the yard and phased through the gate.

"Mr. Conflick!" Sett shouted.

Cliff didn't so much as turn around. Instead, he resembled the delinquent from *The Breakfast Club*, victoriously thrusting his fist into the air. "I'm going to solve this myself!"

Sett and I exchanged a frown. Apparently, we had another sleuth in Bewitcher's Beach. The town was barely big enough for me and Sett, and Cliff's motive was obviously to shift the blame rather than stop the criminal.

CHAPTER 14
BRINGING
THE HEAT

AFTER CLIFF VANISHED, Sett and I went our separate ways. He was supposed to meet the fire marshal to investigate the destruction at her house, and I needed to open Mockbuster for the day.

It took all the willpower I had to sit at my stool behind the register when fires were closing in. Not to mention the unsettling fact that Sett planned to speak with Mae again. At least this time he promised to question Mae at her house rather than at the station. But Sett said he couldn't get there until after five, which gave Cliff more than enough time to create false evidence against the woman he was trying to frame.

For now, I just had to work and wait. Sniffing out a ghost was nearly impossible, and I'd already called Mae. Cliff wasn't there.

The only thing that eased the anxiety buzzing in my belly was talking about movies with customers. Time crawled when the store was empty, but as soon as the bell over the door rang, the clock ticked away too quickly.

Leave before Christmas. The second note also demanded we never come back. The countdown on the threatening note lingered in the back of my mind like a constant cloud that grew heavier and darker with the weight of proverbial rain. A growl rumbled deep in my chest, but I suppressed it and focused on VHS tapes and favorite movies. I had to create my own light. Light that shined brighter when I chatted about movie posters, actors, and the craftsmanship of a plot.

Triton hunched against a movie display and debated over two romantic comedies. I gladly offered my expertise, shifting my mind to happier thoughts.

"If you want something sweet and classy, go with *Emma*," I said. "It's based on a book by Jane Austen, and the old-fashioned setting is a fun escape." I tapped the other video case in his hand and tilted my head side-to-side. "*Four Weddings and a Funeral* is classic too but more drama than cute. Hugh Grant's performance is genius. I hope he stars in more romances."

Despite the details I offered, my input didn't help. Triton forced a long breath through circled lips and weighed both movies, lifting and lowering his hands as if the VHS tapes would feel distinct from one another. "That's a toughie. The drama keeps me hooked, but the funeral side gives me the creeps after all these murders. Now there's fires too."

I couldn't blame him. "I've got an idea!" I shuffled further down the aisle and snagged a more recent movie. "This is what you want. *While You Were Sleeping* has some light drama because the guy's in a coma, but the romance centers around Christmas and family. Very feel-good."

Triton's pimpled face split into a goofy grin, and he swiped the VHS tape from my hands. "Rad!"

Once I returned the other two movies to their respective places, I followed him to the register. I scanned his Mockbuster rewards card, the bag of M&Ms he tossed onto the desk, and the movie. I clicked the case, double-checking the correct VHS tape was inside and that it was rewound and ready for watching.

"So are you and the sheriff close to catching this fire-happy chump? It's why I need a pick-me-up." He pointed at the VHS tape. "To get my mind off all the crime." He'd conjured up the same idea as me.

With a sigh, I put his purchases into a bag of thin plastic and lifted the bag over the desk. "I hate to be the bearer of bad news, but we're not quite sure yet."

"You know, I came to Bewitcher's Beach because it was one of the safest places I'd ever heard of. I did research on crime statistics and whatnot," he said, taking the bag but making no move to leave. "Came all the way from New York City to California because my Nana said the Steel family and Governor Gorch were the best in the business at keeping citizens safe. And that was way back during her time in the sixties. I was mugged once, in New York, you know? I couldn't bear it again, so I moved all the way here, and I'm grateful Steel took over for his father. But it doesn't seem he's as good as his ol' pop with fighting crime, and without the protection spell..." He blew out a breath and shook his head.

"We need him to be the best," I finished for him. "I hear you, and I heard Mayor Fitz is going to target crime in his policies, so hopefully that will make a dent in these troubles."

"Right you are," he said with a small salute. "And we're lucky to have a wolf who can sniff out the big bad pigs." A mix of sandalwood and a hint of happiness' citrus confirmed Triton's words. He had a heap of confidence in me and my nose. But Cliff was trickier than the criminals I'd sniffed out before.

"I think you have that phrase backward," I said. "In the fable, the wolf is the big bad."

"Ah, I guess you're right," he said. "Well, it's wrong in this case!"

"Thanks, Triton," I said, waving as he pushed through the door.

It *was* wrong in my case. I wouldn't hurt a fly, but it took many years for some people to stop fearing those of us with particular *abilities*. That was where hunters came in. Hunters didn't like that werewolves could run faster than them, or that vampires never died, or that witches had magic. Thankfully, hunters were as rare as an unrented new release on a Friday night.

I shook thoughts of spooky hunters and stalking criminals away with a wiggle. Glancing at the clock on the back wall, I repeated what Triton said. "Me and the sheriff..."

It was about that time. Sett would be headed to Mae's house to question her soon. Did Cliff find other ways to frame her? Did he create more fake proof to get Sett to arrest her? I needed to be there, to be the advocate for my friend before Sett was forced to put her in handcuffs. If nothing else, I could smell Mae's truthfulness and report the lavender scent to Sett.

Uncertainty bubbled in my stomach. I hopped around the register desk to the wall of snacks and snagged a bag of Cracker Jack. Plastic crinkled in my tense grip. I popped the caramel-drizzled popcorn into my mouth and munched as I hurried to Everland Theater. With Bette covering Mockbuster, I could keep the store open for regular hours and still support Mae. Plus, Bette wanted the cash to develop pictures and pay for her photography hobby. Since the pups had been spending so much time with Grandmae for the holidays, Bette rarely had a chance for after-school babysitting. Even now, the pups were busy at an ice skating birthday party for their classmate Noodle, and Bette missed out on that few extra bucks.

With the ghost posting up at the shop, I slipped out of

Mockbuster and power-walked to the other side of town. Beyond the suburban neighborhood and Bewitcher's Beach Elementary, land opened to a wide space where houses sat spread apart on multiple acres. Some of the rural folks tended to orchards and small farms on the border while others simply preferred the forest creatures over the bustle of town. I presumed Stevie would live out here when she grew up, befriending foxes and field mice and finches.

For Mae, she lived on the outskirts because the long daily walk into town kept her and Wallace young and fit. Long walk indeed. They probably had to wake before the crack of dawn to make it into the hub of Bewitcher's Beach when the shops opened.

The pavement that surrounded the suburban houses came to an end. Dust kicked up around my shoes from the chalky dirt road. Mae's mansion—as the pups called it—was the last house on Hollow Lane. It was wedged between a forest on the right and vineyards on the left and was a good jaunt away from the orchards. If I went from power-walking to running, I might arrive before the sun dipped below the horizon and shrouded Bewitcher's Beach in darkness.

And before Sett arrived.

Gravel crunched with every hurried step. My lungs heaved, keeping up with my pace and surprisingly not burning. Apparently, step aerobics was good for more than stress relief. My legs didn't tire as easily while in human form, and I kept my breath steady enough.

Bright light flooded Hollow Lane, casting a stream of white on the dirt and gravel with only the shape of my body creating a shadow. I twisted and threw my hands up to shield my eyes. Jogging, I dodged to the side of the road in the weeds, but the car was rolling slowly. Very slowly.

Unease roiled in my belly, and I squinted, trying to make

out the license plate or color of the car, but the headlights were too blinding. The car dropped to a crawl as it advanced. I instinctively stepped away from the road and into the grapevines. Branches stabbed at my back, prodding my blood pressure to rise. Cliff couldn't drive a car, but I'd yet to prove he was the one to write the notes. And as suspicious as he was, why would he use Oyster Inn stationery?

My ears folded back. Had the note bully followed me out here? Claws sprouted from my fingernails and fur started to replace hair. I was a second away from shifting to wolf form and sprinting into the forest when I saw the rectangular lights on top of the car. The red and blue bulbs were not lit, but the police vehicle was indistinguishable.

Sett drove up just as my claws and fur receded and I gulped a fresh breath. The window rolled down, and his elbow rested at the bottom of the frame. "Noema?" I offered a little wave and a tight smile. "Are you going to Mae's to stop me from questioning her?"

"Not to stop you," I said, lifting my nose into the air. *And you'd better not try to stop* me. "Merely to smell the truth."

He chuckled and waved me over. "Get in. I'll drive you the rest of the way."

Just when I thought my pulse would return to normal, my heart stuttered. Fear melted away, but the reality of riding side-by-side in Sett's car replaced it with fizzing nerves and skipping heartbeats. The last time I was in the police car with Sett, we were at a stakeout. We'd spent the entire night sharing snacks, inches apart, when I fell asleep on his shoulder.

I climbed into the passenger seat and twisted to face him, my cheeks flaring as hot as the arsonist's fires. Did he remember how I'd drooled on his shirt and snored at his side? I hadn't slept as well since.

But Sett wasn't looking at me. He leaned over the steering wheel, eyes narrowed and lips parted. "Is that smoke?"

I followed his line of sight through the windshield. *Oh no...* My gut twisted. A thin trail of black puffs lifted into the sky.

"Mae's house," I breathed.

"Seatbelt," he said, pointing to the restraint by my seat. Without another word or a second lost, he shifted the car into drive and slammed the gas pedal.

CHAPTER 15
DEAD END

SETT WALKED SLOWLY, investigated slowly, even ate slowly, but he drove like a bat out of hell. The back of my head bounced off the cushion of the headrest from the whiplash. With one hand on the steering wheel, his other hand groped for the police radio that he used to call the fire department. I prayed they'd arrive fast enough to save Mae, Wallace, and their home. If not, I'd go in and drag them out myself—and Sett better not stop me.

I dared glance at him as if he could read my dangerous thoughts, because I knew if I went in, he'd be right there backing me up. No way would I risk seeing him trapped in another burning building.

Gravel spun and kicked up dirt beneath the tires. A cloud of dust swirled around the car when he slammed to a stop in Mae's driveway. Smoke billowed from beside the Victorian mansion's cylinder brick tower. The two-story house, a decadent red and with a steep tiled rooftop and bay windows, was the envy of Bewitcher's Beach. But it wouldn't be gorgeous much longer. Heavy grief tugged like a stone tied around my heart. The pups would be devastated to hear their Grandmae's home was ruined.

But there was hope. The fire wasn't as wild as it was at the fire marshal's house. Yet. Thick plumes rose up around the base on the left as flames crawled up the side. The blaze crackled and consumed the vines that encompassed the curve of the tower. Most of the smoke puffed up from the wildflowers and weeds covering the ground around the tower's base.

When I spotted Mae standing outside, air filled my lungs. We spilled out of either side of the car, hurrying to reach her.

Mae spun around and slapped her hand to her chest, her other arm crooked with Babette nestled safely against her ribs. The poodle nearly blended into her sweater, camouflaged by the fluffy white fabric. My gaze roved over Mae, scanning for burns as I held my breath. Thankfully, the half-dragon's skin was thick and scaled beneath the visible flesh and resistant to fire—though not fireproof.

"Is Wallace inside?" I asked. My voice squeaked breathlessly as we jogged to her.

Mae reached out, hooking her free arm around my neck and drawing me in for a brief hug. "Oh no, Honey, he's fine. He's Christmas shopping for me at Chanel's boutique." When she released me, a gleaming smile flickered over her face, but it didn't last. "Don't tell him I know he's having her design matching ocean-shaded shawls for me and Babette."

"Are you okay?" Sett asked.

"Shaken." Her quivering hand confirmed it as she gingerly dragged it over Babette's fur.

"Did you see anybody nearby?"

"Yes, Cliff Conflick was floating through those trees." She pointed at the fence that flanked the right side of her property. "He flashed in here from over by the woods. His body passed right through the fence poles..." The rest of her explanation was a jumble of background noise as my heart pounded in my ears.

Cliff. I knew it. This had to count as definitive proof.

"I saw him coming through the kitchen window while I was washing dishes, but he turned and high-tailed it about the same time I smelled the smoke. Thank the heavens Babette was already at her doggie door to bark at him. I scooped her right up and came outside. If she was a guard dog, I'd have sicked her on him! No doubt he was coming to harass me, and I've had enough of it. If he comes back, he'll be sorry."

"Did you get a threat?" I asked.

She nodded, hand to her heaving chest. "Just last night. Wallace found it when he took Babette home and waited for Sett to release me. But I didn't say anything. I thought it'd look suspicious." Her red eyes flashed back-and-forth between us. "Right after I was questioned, a strange note appeared on my very own door. And everyone knows I write the newspaper, especially after Mayor Fitz brought attention to it during his speech last night. Maybe they think I'd written the notes too."

Months ago, Mae had written about Cliff's murder in *The Bewitcher's Beach Gazette.* Another tie to him. Or should I say, tether?

The wail of the fire truck's siren split through the air. Thanks to the Victorian brick, the flames were slow to burn, unable to catch on the brick and mortar. But the fire had caught on the climbing vines that snaked up the tower and reached the shingled roof. There, it blazed with more fervor, and I prayed the firefighters could stop it before the roof was ruined.

I gave Mae's arm a squeeze. "Don't worry about the last tradition being at your house. We can make the popcorn garlands with the kids at Everland Theater when you're up for it."

"Right now?" A gleam twinkled in her eye. "I need a pick-me-up. Maybe a splash of something strong in the cider I'd planned to make." A smile tugged at my lips. Maybe all those aerobics classes with Miss Raven rubbed an extra dose of positivity into Mae. "Oh, but we can't exclude Wallace. So not yet."

I squinted at the base of the tower where foliage was plentiful. The climbing vines were only on the tower, not the rest of the house, and it seemed the arsonist had observed that too. They knew the brick wouldn't burn, but the plants and wooden roof would. One deep whiff told me the culprit used gasoline to douse the weeds and wildflowers, making the greens catch flame easier. Nausea twisted my gut. There was no question this was both intentional and connected to the other fires.

Gravel crunched under the fire truck as it rolled through the gates and sped toward the house. The driver pulled it to a halt by the tower and the fire marshal hopped out the back, hose in hand. They quickly went to work spewing the flames with a gush of water sucked straight from the truck's tank. Though the damage was lessened with every second that passed, my anger grew.

Sett questioned Mae regarding what she saw and heard and every detail about where she was before the fire started. To my alert ears, the questions sounded too close to an accusation when the answer was right in front of his face.

"Thank you, Mae." He gave her an appreciative nod, but it only served to irritate me further. Why was he standing around like a rock stuck in the mud when Cliff was right around the corner? "I'd like to continue this conversation after I've spoken with the fire marshal."

"Why?" I blurted.

Sett's brow spiked, and he crossed his arms. "Because it's my job—"

"Nuh-uh. No. *Curses!* Sett, don't you see? Cliff threatened me. He's been harassing Mae, and he was on her property when the fire started!" The words spilled out, rivaling the deafening blast of water gushing from the fire hose. "What more proof do you need?"

Sett cupped my elbow and led me away from Mae, who was busy calming Babette. The poodle didn't like my outburst and yapped ferociously, riled by my nervous energy. Shushing and rocking her, Mae treated the tiny dog like a crying baby.

Sett leveled with me, narrowed eyes stern and grip on my arm firmly. "I hear you, Noema. I do. But the danger is here, which is where a protector of the people belongs. Nothing about what Mae witnessed is evidence of Cliff starting the fire. She said he was on that side of the property, opposite from the fire."

"Or she was just shaken and can't recall every detail. Cliff could be off trying to set another fire. Clearly Mae wouldn't set her own house on fire, so I don't see the point in questioning her."

His wings flickered, expanding slightly and then tightening against his back. "The *point* is to get a more complete picture. Have you ever tried to solve a puzzle without the picture on the box? Or cook a new meal without the recipe?"

"Yes, in fact—" My jaws snapped shut at the look on his face. Sett's brow was stretched a mile high and his gray lips pursed, exaggerating the line of his cheekbones. Not for one second did he believe me.

"You don't cook."

"I was referring to the puzzle part, thank you very much. I've tried a jigsaw puzzle without the picture because my kids lost the box. I was sick of the pieces lying around, so I went wild on it."

"But did you complete it?"

Silence. It was all I could offer him because I didn't want to confess that my impatience and lack of a picture made the puzzle nearly impossible. I ended up throwing all the pieces away.

Looking over his shoulder, Sett cleared his throat. I followed his line of sight to see the brick still stood and the roof was intact. Only a small section of the shingles were charred. The climbing vine was disintegrated, and the gasoline-soaked foliage was nothing more than a withered black spot on the earth now.

"It looks like the damage is under control." He spoke without facing me. "Let me check in with the fire marshal and then..." He twisted his neck and met my gaze again, expression softened this time. If stone skin could soften. It could crack and he could bleed just like everyone else, but sometimes it was hard to believe Sett had any sensitivity. Especially when he treated every case as a set of facts and numbers and policies. "Then we'll find Cliff."

WHILE HE FINISHED BUSINESS, I wrapped a comforting arm around Mae's shoulder. She was shaken but had calmed quickly, only worried about her baby Babette now. Carefully, she crouched to let the dog jump from her arms, and then she excused herself for a walk to "ease Babette's nerves."

With the flames gone, shadow shrouded the rural property. Mae had yet to turn on the porch light for the evening, and the road beyond had no street lamps. The woods and weeds were dark but also serene and quiet enough to clear my head. Maybe a walk would calm my nerves too. Pacing around the mansion, I examined it for leftover cigarettes, an abandoned lighter, anything suspicious. Back at the front, I avoided eye contact with the fire marshal and Sett, keeping myself from interrupting them. I slipped past them and carefully sniffed around the brick tower. The gasoline stench was pungent enough to burn my nose and turn my stomach.

Once the investigators finished their discussion and Mae returned, the fire marshal abandoned Sett to speak with Mae.

"Everything okay?" I asked, noting the crease between Sett's brows.

He swallowed hard and eyed Mae. "The fire marshal found pieces of newspaper in the bushes where the fire started. It appears the arsonist used the paper to help the flames spread quicker."

"And?" I prodded. I knew what he was getting at, since Mae reported news in *The Bewitcher's Beach Gazette.* Usually, she only wrote about a missing bicycle or a pesky gopher tearing up the local garden, but since crime came to town, so did serious reports and veiled accusations. As a former criminal herself, Mae wasn't afraid to call out suspicious behavior. She wasn't afraid of anything, really.

"And I'll have to call Mae into the station again to ask her about it." He yanked the passenger door open for me and leaned close to my ear. His breath sent an involuntary shiver through me as he whispered, "And I don't want any harassment from you about it."

I shot him a daggered glare as if he was a ghost and I wielded the magical blade that could send his spirit onward.

He continued, marching to the other side of the vehicle. "If you let me do my job right and she's innocent, everything will be fine."

"Of course she's innocent," I said when he dropped into the seat beside me.

"Of course." He nodded and then pulled the gear in reverse.

When Sett whipped the car around and slammed the gas

pedal, I gripped the handle on the door. The car jolted and bounced along the dirt and gravel, tossing me around like the werewolf-version of a ragdoll. My other hand found his arm where growing claws dug into his rough skin. *Stone skin cracks too.* I yanked my hand back, cringing at the sight of the marks my claws left behind. He didn't seem to notice, only focused ahead as the car barreled through the open gate. The tires screeched to a stop much sooner than I expected.

No. The sound didn't come from the tires. He hit the brakes suddenly, slapping his hands over his ears.

Horrible shrieking ripped through the air like a banshee's scream. I grabbed my long ears and tugged them down, bending and pulling them close to my temples. But it did little to block the painful sound. The shrill scream rang out at the same pitch over and over, only pausing for a second in between long releases.

Dust puffed around us, settling on the windshield and the navy blue hood. Sett shoved through the door, and despite the awful sound, I followed, kicking the passenger door open.

Outside the car, the screeching stopped. Silence fell other than my heaving breaths. The sound rang in my ears, muted but still annoying and a little painful.

"Was that your car?" I asked, letting go of my ears.

Sett shook his head. He scanned the area, and after a minute, we climbed back into the car only to find the source— or at least the spot—of the scream.

"Will it stop if you keep driving?" I asked, desperate to speed away from the ache in my ears.

"I told you, it's not the car—"

"Just try it!"

Sett hit the gas and we lurched forward. The sound vanished as quickly as it had descended upon us.

"Told you."

Halting the car again, he shoved through the door and tossed a rebuttal over his shoulder. "It's not the car."

"What are you doing?"

"I can't ignore a cry for help."

"You think someone's in danger?" When he ignored me and marched back to the spot where he'd stopped the car, I hurried after him.

He stood like a silent sentinel at the edge of Mae and Wallace's property. Finally, shaking his head, he answered my question. "I don't hear it anymore. But it was definitely someone. Or some*thing*. Some of the creatures in these woods have residual magic left over from witches who lived here. I've heard a robin speak German—"

His voice dropped away, and he slapped his hands to his ears at the same time he squeezed his eyes shut.

"Sett?" Before I could ask if he was okay, the sound assaulted me again. My teeth grated, and I shut my eyes as if the darkness could block the horrible sound. After a pause, the screams repeated, and I couldn't handle it any longer. I jumped back, ready to spin and run to the car. But the sound was gone.

I'd stepped into silence.

My wolf ears peaked, angling outward. With a step forward, the shrieking returned. I jumped back again, this time grabbing Sett's arm and tugging him with me. "The sound is only right in this one spot." I waved my hand in a circle over a brush of weeds.

Right on the edge of Mae's property.

"I was right," he breathed.

"Excuse me?"

Sett glanced down at me. "It's a cry for help. There are words in the scream."

"What?" He waved for me to step forward again, and I vehemently shook my head. "With these wolf ears? Are you kidding me?" How could he hear words through the screeching? I could barely hear my own thoughts.

Instead of encouraging me to see for myself, he braved the sound again, firmly planting his feet on the patch of weeds. He stood frozen, eyes closed, listening. His lips twisted to a grimace, and he stepped back.

His eyes opened, but he didn't look my way. "It's Cliff's voice."

Thoughts of Hattie's explanation swirled around my head. This was a scar. A ringing or screeching left behind from a spirit stabbed by a ghost blade. And given a ghost couldn't wield it itself, someone had to have stabbed him...

My hand shot to my mouth, but it didn't stop the words from spilling out. "He was killed."

Sett nodded. "With a ghost blade."

And the only person wealthy enough to afford a black market blade was the woman who owned half the town's buildings...

He shuffled through the weeds, tugging a handkerchief from his coat pocket. Crouching, he retrieved an object from among the greenery. Pinched between his thumb and forefinger under the flimsy fabric, the silver hilt of a blade caught the glint of the moon.

The ghost blade was exactly as I'd pictured. Small with a black jagged blade, and though the edges were rough, the shine was impeccable—sharpened on Cliff's spirit. Bile stained my tongue with a bitter taste and dread slammed into my gut, weighted with worry for my friend. The weapon was right here, at the corner of Mae's property.

His eyes slid to me and my mouth dropped open. "No." I protested what he had yet to even say. "No way. Mae would never."

"I know. She's not a killer. But she did threaten him, and the weapon is in her yard..."

His voice faded from my ears. The facts faded from my mind. Jargon like "probable cause" and "arrest" faded from my attention.

Enough of waiting for Sett's protocol. I silently swore to Mae, to Wallace, and even to my pups that I'd track down the real criminal and absolve their Grandmae of this heinous accusation once and for all.

CHAPTER 16
LIKE WILDFIRE

NOT TWO HOURS later at the police station, I found myself pacing a hole in front of Sett's desk. I didn't have to like his slow process to work as a team. I'd use every resource at my disposal. Two brains were better than one—another one of Mayor Fitz's cliche sayings itched in my mind.

Despite the warm, melt-in-your-mouth flaky biscuit on my tongue, I only tasted bitterness. I swiped a mug of steaming mulled cider from the desk and downed the drink. The warm liquid seared all the way through my throat and didn't settle well in my stomach. Cinnamon should have mingled delightfully with the savory biscuit, but everything lost its flavor. With Mae returned to number one on the list of suspects, I didn't have a taste for Christmas. Not even Sett's homemade goods could fill the pit in my gut.

I stared at the culprit—the awful man who dared accuse my babies' Grandmae. Okay, Sett wasn't awful, but I had to direct the flood of nerves and anger and confusion somewhere.

Sett sat hovering over his desk with his hands propping up his head. The plate of biscuits and the mug beside him remained untouched. Butter melted into the fluffy cream texture, and steam coiled from the cider. In front of him was a notepad with dozens of scribbles. Sett's indecipherable handwriting covered the lined page, and a large red blot of ink crossed out the note in the margin that read *Mae Wildefyre: ghost blade on property, reporting columnist, at the Aerobics Alive during the fire, change in insurance.*

A minute before, I'd grabbed the notepad and a red marker from Sett's desk to remove my friend's name from his list of suspects. Of course, crossing it out did nothing to release Mae from behind bars where she currently sat with her own plate of biscuits and mug of cider.

"It doesn't make sense that she'd risk her own house," I said, taking another tasteless bite of the biscuit. I forced the thick chewy lump down my throat.

"It doesn't. And to play devil's advocate, she could have known that brick doesn't burn and the fire wouldn't do much damage to the structure."

"But it destroyed her husband's ivy!"

"I know, Noema." Sett sighed and rubbed at his temples. "Someone is probably framing her, but I can't release her with this much evidence stacked against her."

"It's sick," I spat. "Do you even realize it's Christmastime?" After I spun, I wanted to bite back the words. Of course he realized. The station was decorated with twinkling lights. A wreath hung in the window, and a small pine tree with shiny silver and red bulbs brightened the front corner. The cider he left warming in the crock pot had an extra dash of cinnamon for the holiday, and he originally baked these biscuits for another Christmas movie night at Everland Theater. An event that was now canceled thanks to the arsonist.

When I turned to him again, my ears folded back and I couldn't meet his eyes. His silence was enough. If only I could take back the words I spewed.

"I'm sorry." My voice was small and tight. I stared at the notes. Though they were upside down from my point of view and barely more than chicken scratch, I made out the words. *Arsonist's targets: deputy, Miss Raven, Judy Knovel, the coroner, fire marshal, Crow, Noema Wolf. And Mae,* I added. What did each of us have in common? The coroner, Mae, and I had been involved in crime before, either reporting or investigating it. But Miss Raven and Judy didn't match that criteria. And would the arsonist come after me next? If they did, could I use myself as bait and catch them in the act?

All I had to do was set a trap. But I had to set it sooner rather than later, before the arsonist caught wind of Mae's arrest. I doubted this crafty criminal was stupid enough to set another fire while she was already blamed and behind bars. The act would essentially clear her name and turn focus back to the investigation.

Could I convince the arsonist I had evidence of their crime? That would certainly make them come running.

After clearing my throat, I lifted my chin and wagged my finger at him. "You know what? The mayoral debate is tomorrow. The whole town will be there. I can talk to everyone and see what they've seen and heard."

"Noema—"

"What? You can't stop me from chatting with my friends and neighbors." I took another swig of cider, finally tasting the sweet apple flavor with a twinge of tangy orange and spicy cinnamon. "And you definitely can't stop me from trying to get Grandmae out of jail. That's just a fact."

Sett's eyes dropped, distant and staring at nothing. Unless that particular patch of floor was suddenly interesting. His Adam's apple bobbed with a hard swallow before he spoke. "I'll be talking with everyone as well."

"Good," I said. I sucked down the last of the cider in my

cup before returning it to Sett's desk. It hit the desktop a little too hard. The ceramic didn't crack, but I cringed.

His eyes rolled up to meet mine. As if he knew what I had planned, his eyes narrowed to suspicious slits.

Of course I wasn't just going to make small talk with soccer moms and business owners. I was going to drop hints that I had evidence stored at Mockbuster and that the shop would be empty that same night—empty and an easy target for attack. I was going to lie to everyone because I'd be right there lying in wait to see the arsonist's face when they came to destroy the so-called evidence.

THE NEXT EVENING, crime was the talk of the town. Thanks to Mayor Fitz, everyone carried a whiff of hope that the dangers in Bewitcher's Beach would soon be squelched. Hope was a delectable scent that mixed excitement's banana cream pie with the lemon lime tart of happiness. The result replicated the smell of key lime pie's citrus meringue. I soaked in the smell, taking a huge sniff of the surrounding air that swirled around the listening crowd.

Sirens, fairies, gargoyles, and humans alike stood in the park before the temporary platform. A large banner was tacked to the front of the small stage that said *A vote for me is a vote for security!* Dr. Pitt didn't have a banner, but he spoke with reverence and inspiration. Everyone absorbed Mayor Fitz's words too, entranced by his wide grin and uplifting message. Even vampires attended the speeches thanks to the fact that they'd scheduled the event after the sun went down.

I scanned the sea of faces. Cliff was blatantly absent... Knots twisted my stomach.

I tore my eyes from the people and faced the man whose hope fueled theirs. Street lamps shined off Mayor Fitz's smooth head, and a massive smile split his face. Promises spilled from his mouth, sweetening the deal if we chose to vote for him again.

I licked my lips, nearly tasting the palpable hope. Hope that what he said was in our future. A sudden craving for key lime pie struck me, and I made a little promise of my own. *Ask Sett for a recipe later.* Not that I cooked or baked. Ever. But maybe with Sett's help... *No.* After I cleared Mae's name, I wanted space from Sett.

A tall, dark, and handsome figure caught the corner of my left eye. I did a double-take and gasped. "Crow!"

"Missed ya," he said, grinning. "And I couldn't help but wonder who'd win this debate." I squeezed his hand and allowed him to listen. Within a minute, he became enraptured by Mayor Fitz's mesmerizing positivity. A little grin even curled at the corner of Crow's lips where the hook of the scythe-shaped scar tugged.

"We'll be so busy enjoying festivals, plays, and holidays that even visitors at Bewitcher's Beach won't have time for crime!" Mayor Fitz bellowed. He thrust a finger in the air, inspiring scattered claps.

Crow dipped his head close to mine, bringing with him the cool scent of forests and soil and the freshness of the earth after a heavy rain. "Count me out for all that. One big event a month is plenty."

"Seriously," I said with a snort. "As if I'm not already busy enough." How could I manage making every day as special as the holidays for my pups?

He nudged me with his elbow, and his rakish grin resembled a crescent moon. "Hey, do you think if we're just chillin' and not running from party to festival that Fitz will consider us criminals?"

A laugh popped out of me, and I rolled my eyes. "More like he'll just consider us total buzz kills."

Mayor Fitz's voice pricked my ears again. He'd grabbed the microphone and started walking the stage with it like a celebrity comedian. "I'm currently in discussion with the folks at the state capitol. I'm looking at hiring new law enforcement officers for the security of Bewitcher's Beach."

Minimal claps scattered through the mass of Bewitched citizens. Those who didn't cheer were likely thinking of the protection spell. If we reinstated the blanket of magic that once resided over our town, we wouldn't need more than Sheriff Sett to patrol our streets. Did he know about this? Sett wasn't exactly used to working with a team of officers. Of course, if he needed help guarding the town, he wouldn't turn it away either.

Dr. Pitt said his piece on the matter, but Mayor Fitz wasn't done yet. Interrupting his opponent wasn't a good look. The mayor yanked the microphone's wire alongside him as he paced with a confident gait. "We once relied on a protection spell as a safety net to shelter our people, but that has failed us."

Failed? More like was stolen. Stripped. Destroyed. As far as I knew, the magic never failed to stop attacks before it was mysteriously removed.

"But I will not fail you! Today, in December of 1997, I make *you*, you beautiful Bewitched citizen, this promise." He pointed a stubby finger at a pixie in the front of the crowd and then shifted his attention to a human on the other side. "And you. And you in the back!" His aim landed on Crow. People cheered but not as loudly as they had for Dr. Pitt's answer.

Crow shot me a mischievous look and whispered, "Just as I thought. No chillin' allowed. He's already got his eye on me." A laugh bubbled from him, but the mayor's speech drowned him out.

"The protection spell was our old line of defense, and we mourn its loss. But modern problems require modern solutions. So I say, 'out with the old and in with the new'!" Cheering deafened me. Through the noise, I caught Mayor Fitz's final and repetitive promise that was quickly turning into a catchphrase. "I'll stop crime in no time!"

After the speech ended, Mayor Fitz took a seat on the edge of the platform and beamed at the circle of citizens that surrounded him. They fired questions and compliments his way, and he responded cheerfully. I flicked my ears to the side, hoping to shift my hearing to the conversations around me.

"Are you down to grab a burger?" Crow shoved his hands into his pockets and nodded toward the towering milkshake in the distance. He rolled from his heels to the balls of his feet. Impatient and entirely too much like me when I was eager for a response. Though I usually opted to tap my foot.

"I'm going to linger and mingle," I said, swirling my finger around to gesture at everyone socializing.

"That's cool. I'm going to bounce though, I'm starving."

"Bounce?" I teased, a smile sneaking onto my face. "You've really gone all-in with the slang. Am I even *cool* enough to hang out with you?"

He smirked and then leaned in for a quick kiss on the cheek. When he pulled back, midnight eyes meeting mine, he said, "You're cooler. I'm just the dork at the roller rink. But hey, I've been thinking about you staying at Mockbuster. After that note and with the fires getting more frequent, I was thinking you should bunk at my hotel room." My cheeks burned. Sleep in Crow's hotel room? I couldn't. We were barely dating. "I only have the one bed—"

"Crow!" I punched him in the shoulder.

"I was going to say, I only have the one bed, so you take it and I'll sleep on the couch. I love falling asleep to the X-Files theme song, and I know you're a fan of the show. So it's a win-win."

Hair prickled on the back of my neck and I glanced to either side, catching sight of Celeste, Triton, and Chanel looking at us. Apparently, I'd shouted Crow's name louder than I'd thought. Punching him probably sealed the deal. A lover's spat was always more interesting than idle chit chat. An idea surged, and prickling shifted to a rush of adrenaline. I could use this attention to my advantage.

"I just want you to be safe," Crow continued.

"Actually," I said, as loudly as possible. "The arsonist isn't a threat to me anymore. I have evidence that I'll be turning in tomorrow. The criminal will be arrested first thing in the morning. But I'd still like to spend the night with you. A little getaway at a hotel sounds perfect. Mockbuster is lonely without the kids, anyway." I was laying it on about as thick as the mayoral candidates. I resisted the urge to glance at the surrounding crowd and be sure they were still eavesdropping. Thankfully, I didn't need to.

Chanel swooped in with a ballerina's grace and flashed a dazzling smile of white teeth. The siren had taken the bait, and behind her, Celeste and Triton eagerly watched. "Forgive me, but I couldn't help overhearing that the investigation has made progress. Do tell." She wiggled her perfectly shaped brows arched over doe eyes the color of the ocean. "What evidence do you have?"

Curses. I didn't think that part through. What evidence could I claim? A DNA sample from the crime scenes? No, I wasn't a detective or a forensic specialist.

But I *was* the owner of a video rental store where we also sold packs of empty tapes to record home videos. Plus, my son was seen on more than one occasion carrying around our family's camcorder. "A video," I said, finally satisfying her curiosity. The scent of my own guilt stunk up the place. I didn't like having to lie to a friend, but Chanel was sure to spread the news. In fact, it was already working. A nearby couple and a family of gargoyles had tuned into our conversation, as evident by their watchful eyes. "I predicted which building they'd torch next and set up my camcorder. I caught 'em in the act. The whole crime is on video. It's not a perfect shot, but I believe Sett will be able to identify them. All I have to do is turn it over to him so he can lock them up."

"So what are you waiting for?" Chanel waved her mani-cured hands, gesturing for me to run off toward Mockbuster.

"The tape got stuck in the deck," I said. This wasn't a lie. The tapes got stuck in our camcorder all the time, and if I pulled too hard to get them out, the film got caught and unrav-eled or ripped. I shot Crow a look, hoping I wouldn't regret roping him into my deception. "I was waiting for Crow to finish fixing it."

His mouth twitched in the flash of a grimace. It was an obvious lie, and he'd just caught me red-handed.

I forced a smile. "I can't risk the tape getting ruined."

Chanel hummed and slid her gaze back and forth between us. "Good luck to you both. Mind if I share the good news? Just with the other moms in my boys' preschool class? To settle their nerves."

"Just them," I agreed. Of course I knew that wouldn't be the case. And requesting they keep it concealed would only help the rumor spread faster. The more it appeared to be a secret, the juicier the tidbit sounded. Before the crowd even dispersed, I had no doubt every single Bewitched would know that I had a tape of evidence at Mockbuster.

As soon as she walked away, Crow stepped closer, and I forced myself to look up at him.

"You were lying," he said.

"Am I that obvious?"

"Remember when we played Uno that night at the roller rink? I realized you have a tell. Whenever I asked if you were going to wreck my game and put down a Draw Four or Plus Two, it came out." The memory was light, but his tone didn't match and his usual smirk didn't accompany the words. "Your claws."

He pointed to my hands. I flipped them over, noticing the barest hint of pointed tips growing from my fingernails. Apparently the unease of lying sent me into defense mode. Claws and fur were always the first to appear before I'd drop to all fours in my wolf form. "It was easier to catch when you were holding cards."

"I'm sorry, Crow."

"Is this an investigation tactic I'm not privy to? Something you and Sett set up?"

My claws grew a little longer, and unease buzzed in my chest. "Something like that."

He only nodded, silent for a minute. "Okay, well, I'm assuming the entire bit was a lie and that you're not going to the hotel with me?"

I shook my head and offered an apologetic frown. "Are you mad?" The question slipped out. I didn't smell any angry smoke from him, but among this many people, deciphering one person's emotions was tricky.

He narrowed his eyes, making me wait before reaching out to tuck a loose curl behind my ear. "No. If investigating makes you feel safe, then..." He paused just long enough for the ghost of a smirk to return. "You go girl."

A laugh popped out of me, and the buzzing in my ribcage quieted. "More slang? I'm definitely not hip enough for you."

Suddenly his lips flattened and eyes darkened. He stepped closer to me, our noses inches apart. I held my breath as if a hot and heavy kiss was coming my way. "Listen, if these investigations ever get dangerous, you'll back off, right?"

"More promises?" I joked, trying to make light of it. I glanced at the stage and tossed my thumb toward Mayor Fitz. He'd hopped off the stage, leaning on it to chat with people in the crowd. "I think Mayor Fitz made enough of those for one night."

Crow didn't laugh.

A strained moment passed, and he stepped back, putting distance between us again. "Sett's not the only one who wants to protect you."

With that, he turned and stalked away into the crowd. I didn't have time to dwell on this strange rivalry. Could I blame Crow for the hint of jealousy he left in the air? I'd spent a lot of time with Sett lately.

I picked my way through Bewitched cliques, catching pieces of their conversations as I ducked out of the park. The continual rise of hope smothered me with too much key lime pie. Too tart now. Too sweet—if that was possible. As I looked around, my own hope swelled and peaked the scent to near-nauseating levels.

My plan worked. Every group, every family, every neighbor and friend were already discussing what the tape might reveal. *Who did Noema's camcorder catch on video?* Too bad I couldn't answer that now.

If only the tape was real...

CHAPTER 17
SMILE FOR THE CAMERA

IF THE TAPE was real and the culprit caught on camera, I wouldn't be pacing the shadowed back aisles of Mockbuster in the middle of the night. Alone.

I balanced Halen's heavy black camcorder in my right palm and kept it pointed toward the windowed walls that lined the front of the shop. If the creep showed up to get the fake tape, I'd catch him *on* tape. With the red recording light on, I kept my eyes trained on the door while staying hidden in the dark corner by the less-than-popular western movies display. Sleep tugged at my heavy lids, but fluttering nerves kept me upright and ears perked.

Once the arsonist showed their face on film, I'd run to Sett with proof. Then he'd have to release Mae. That was, if I could refrain from wolfing out and tackling the criminal as soon as they showed up.

Their crime had split up families. I missed my pups though they were just next door with Hattie and Bette. Mae and Wallace were spending the night apart. As many traditions and magical holiday experiences I tried to create, it wasn't enough because my kids might not have Christmas with their Grand-mae. *Curses.* I really missed them.

A thick lump strained my throat. I hated that we were all split up. Hopelessness dissolved as a smoky smell swirled around me. My anger built into resolve.

Movement outside sent my heart skipping. My ears folded back, and a growl rumbled in my belly. Though I opted for intimidation, the claws and fur sprouting from my fingernails and flesh revealed the nerves beneath.

A leaf danced across the sidewalk and disappeared from view. All at once, my muscles melted and eyes grew heavy again. It was nothing more than the remnants of autumn floating by. The sidewalk was empty, and quiet blanketed the park beyond. I glanced at the clock.

4:17 am.

I blinked sleep away and willed the pounding in my chest to slow. Could I hold myself back when this creep showed their face? The receding claws and vanishing fur said otherwise. A mere leaf in the wind nearly had me dropping to all fours.

"I need to calm down," I whispered to a snoozing Squeaks.

When he didn't respond, I drifted from the darkness to the row of family films. My comfort movies never failed to shine light on the shadows. *The Borrowers, The Sandlot, The Mighty Ducks.* Each film was like magic to my soul. I traced the VHS tapes as though I'd soak up the soothing story from the tape itself.

It worked. For a little while. Until another leaf blew by or a dying bulb in a street lamp flickered, causing me to jump. At least I was ready and aware. The arsonist had caught wind of the rumor, of that I was sure. It was the talk of the entire town before I'd even made it out of the park after the speech.

Every tick, tick, ticking minute was tedious.

Early morning remained dark, boring, quiet. Only our

breathing and the passage of time broke the long stretches of silence.

I finally took a seat on the floor in the corner next to Squeaks. There, I had a view of the front window, but the shadow shrouded me in privacy. A yawn overcame me, and as soon as I snapped my jaw shut, a dark figure approached.

My heart was a jumble of erratic beats, and anticipation sucked my breath away. The figure stalked through the park, headed this direction. They wore dark clothing with a hood pulled over their head, creating a shadow that blocked their face.

I didn't move a muscle, not even to breathe, as they pulled something from their pocket. Was it a cigarette? A lighter? I expected them to carry a jug of gasoline too, but the object was nothing more than a cylinder can.

With every step they took closer to Mockbuster, my pulse ramped, thudding a hundred beats a minute in my ear like a drum. I drew in a slow breath. *Calm. Or you'll wolf out and ruin it.* If my impatience had me tackling them before they committed the crime, I'd never know if they were truly to blame.

The figure hopped onto the sidewalk and marched straight at Mockbuster. Though I knew they couldn't see me, I shrank deeper into the darkness. I bumped the western display and a tape clattered to the floor, almost whacking my head on the way down. I swallowed a yelp and whipped my attention back to the front.

The person froze. Listening. Waiting. And then they shook the can vigorously, and liquid sprayed over Mockbuster's window. My mouth fell open. They weren't setting my business on fire, they were starting with graffiti.

Spray paint curled and dripped as they wrote several big

X's in red across the windows. When they tilted their chin back, their hood slipped off.

My hand shot to my mouth as I stifled another gasp.

A familiar mohawk identified Reed immediately, but lack of sleep had me wondering if I'd dreamed it. Didn't Reed and his father have alibis? I nearly pinched myself to be sure I was awake, but I didn't need to. Reed paused his painting to tug his sleeves to his elbows, revealing the skull tattoo for confirmation. A cigarette almost slipped from his lips when he coughed. He yanked it from his mouth and stomped it into the sidewalk.

As suspected, the criminal showed up after I'd set the bait.

He was marking Mockbuster to be set ablaze. The clues pointed right at him. Cigarettes. Vandalism.

Reed packed up his spray paint into a small backpack and then took off out of view. I darted for the front, peering out the glass to see him striding toward The Oyster Inn. Was he retrieving a lighter to spark a flame? Or gasoline to catch and spread faster?

I scooped Squeaks into my pocket and slipped outside, cursing at the chime of the bell on Mockbuster's door. The camera caught it all, except for the smell. Reed disappeared inside the inn, leaving behind him an unexpected scent. The aroma of banana cream pie swirled in his wake. Excitement? For burning his next target.

A gasp hitched in my throat. It was now or never-seeing-Mockbuster-again. I had to confront Reed and catch him red-handed with the gasoline container and lighter. I marched past Everland Theater and across the alley, stopping in front of the cream and green inn. Since I couldn't very well follow him into his hotel room, I paused, waiting by the lobby's door.

When he showed his face again, he'd have to smile for the camera.

Minutes passed like hours. Crawling. Yawning. Sleepiness

tugged at my eyes and arms, and the camcorder grew heavy in my hands. I hurried around to the back of the inn, just to be sure that door wasn't in use. I couldn't have Reed slipping out into the alley from Barney's office. Though that was unlikely, considering Barney kept his office under lock and key, terrified anyone might muss up his immaculate organization.

Still, I had to be sure.

I jogged to my post by the front door, holding the camcorder close so my clumsiness didn't get the best of me. I was only gone for two minutes at most. Back on the cobblestone, a whiff of smoke stung my nose.

Two minutes too late.

My head whipped in the direction of Mockbuster, and my jaw nearly hit the ground. My shop—my home—was set on fire.

CHAPTER 18
A SLOW BURN

MOCKBUSTER'S BURNING!

Pounding, my heart ran away, but my feet refused to move.

How could I let myself walk away in the first place?

The fire was small, only having caught on the right wall by the snacks and register. Flames scorched the base of the wall, and already the fire truck's siren was blaring through the early morning air.

The next ten minutes were a blur. I used The Oyster Inn's phone to call the fire station. I checked on Squeaks to make sure he hadn't been jarred too hard in my pocket. I stepped on a cigarette abandoned on the sidewalk.

The fire truck screeched to a halt outside Mockbuster, and the rest was a tornado of firefighters, the hose, water. The fire marshal took longer to arrive than her crew, given that she was staying at a hotel outside of town now. But before I knew it, the flames were tamped out and Mockbuster had only suffered minor damage. It was an oasis in the desert of bad news.

That and the fact that I'd caught the culprit.

I thanked the fire marshal and left her to do her job, investigating around Mockbuster. Squeaks opted to stay with her, wanting to supervise and confirm the marshal did her job to his expectations. As if the mouse had any clue how to investigate arson.

I speed-walked across town. With a criminal housed in the jail cell, Sett spent nights at the station. And if he was already alerted by the fire truck's siren, I'd surely pass him on my way there. The sun already peeked over the horizon, casting yolky rays through puffy clouds.

Had Reed marked the building for destruction and then Zed came to do the final deed? Despite the warmth of the sun, my blood chilled.

I needed to clear my mind, so I broke into a sprint, feeling the cool air through my curls as I ran. Exhaustion tugged at my muscles, but I relished the freedom of running and the release of pent-up tension. Nerves and fear melted away, and the fresh breeze alerted me better than a hit of caffeine. But I still craved a breakfast of Diet Pepsi. Yes, a delicious and bubbly Diet Pepsi, Mae's release, and the culprit caught. Despite the almost-tragedy at Mockbuster, today was shaping up to be a good one.

As soon as I shoved through the door, I spotted the tips of Sett's wings. He was barrelling toward me, eyes fixed on the door. I dodged to the side before his hard shoulder smacked into my face.

"Noema!" Breathless, he froze and folded his wings, looking down at me. Concern creased his brow, and his jaw tightened. Knowing passed between us. With his hand absent-mindedly perched right behind his hip where he kept hand-cuffs attached to his belt, I knew he was about to make an arrest. Or at least the thought was on his mind.

We both spoke at the same time. "I have news."

We paused, waiting for the other and then stumbled over

one another's words again. "Mae?" I asked while he said, "Mockbuster?"

We tried to be polite and allow the other person to speak first, but the twitch of his wings and my tapping foot pushed us both to blurt out once again.

"You know?" I said.

"I heard." His gaze flicked to the window. Mockbuster was too far to spot from this corner of town, but I knew what the distant look meant. His brow pinched tighter. "I should have come, but by the time I made it into the park, the fire was already out and I'm in the middle of a break in the investigation. I'm sorry."

The gentle tone soothed me. Too much. My muscles melted, and suddenly the floodgates opened. Something about the softness in his eyes or the sincerity of his apology or the light touch of my arm broke the dam that I didn't know held back a rush of tears. All at once, exhaustion from sleepless nights and shock of the fire and worry for my home spilled out with hot tears over my cheeks.

Sett's touch firmed as he pulled me into him. Thick arms wrapped around me, and my face buried in his chest. Everything about his stony body should have felt rigid and rough, but he was a blanket, soft and gentle and cool enough to relax my raging wolf fever. He wasn't magic, but, for now, he'd become the protection spell. The blanket that kept us all as safe as he could.

The harder I sobbed, the tighter he hugged, and it spiraled into a cycle. His hold squeezed the tears out of me, and the more I gasped and sniffled, the closer he pulled me into him. If he hadn't mentioned a breakthrough, I might have stood there for hours, letting him keep me upright. Letting his navy shirt soak my tears. Letting myself grieve for all the beautiful buildings that made home *home.*

I'd been so caught up in the mystery and catching the arsonist that I didn't even recognize what was buried beneath the surface. Miss Raven's historical building, Judy's cottage, Grandmae's home where the pups were supposed to be spending the night, even the coroner's office was part of the magic of Bewitcher's Beach's familiarity. The place my kids were growing up and making memories. The place I'd found family. Blood or not, Hattie was my sister and Mae the pup's grandmother. The place I met Sett...

I released him and wiped my nose, avoiding his gaze. If I looked into his eyes, the crying would start over and we'd be back to square one. At least crying relieved a bit of the weight tugging at my gut. But now wasn't time for another breakdown —not with a break*through* on the horizon.

"The case?" I squeaked out, intending to say a full sentence but the squeeze in my throat wouldn't allow it.

The ghost of a smile—a smile—actually flickered over Sett's face. "Your VHS tape idea sparked something for me," he said, eyes sparkling with a sudden and unexpected mischief. "The rumor prodded me to look at the security tape from Chanel's shop again." My mouth fell open. Of course Sett would have heard the lie, but I never expected it would help him with the case. "I was stuck. Everything pointed to Mae, but there was no trace of her finances that showed she spent enough money to buy a ghost blade. I'm working on a theory that Cliff witnessed the arsonist, and that's why they attacked him. Cliff was snooping too, hoping to throw the blame off of him, and the criminal probably knew this and didn't want to risk Cliff outing him. How they got the ghost blade so fast, I don't know. Maybe it was insurance, keeping it on hand in case any ghost snuck up on them. Hattie has been known to snoop around with you."

Regret slammed me, quickly filling my nose with the stench of charred toast. I should have been more careful not to get Hattie involved. Though she had enjoyed helping and was plenty tough on her own. "Anyway, I decided to double check Zed since he's come into a load of money recently with Mayor Fitz's remodels. Zed is benefitting a lot more with the rebuilding than Mae will through the insurance claims. In fact, the insurance claims just came through on Aerobics Alive and Judy's house, and they'll barely cover the cost of repairs. Mae and Wallace were planning to dip into their own savings."

My ears, which had been folded back, slowly perked again. I soaked in every bit of good news.

"Reed's face is never actually shown in the video. Zed is visible with a man near him of a similar build, but it doesn't prove Reed's alibi. I should have seen that the first time, but I had to follow where most of the evidence led, and without help, there just isn't time for me to do it all."

Anticipation buzzed in my chest. I bit my lip so I wouldn't interrupt him just to say we'd come to the same conclusion. Zed and Reed could be double arsonists.

"I knew it," I said because I just couldn't help myself. "I swore he came inside Aerobics Alive to talk with Bette during one of the water breaks. He definitely wasn't at Chanel's boutique the whole time." I leaned to one side to see past his shoulder and wing to the back of the station. "Is Mae here?"

"She's at home with Wallace, I assume. Or maybe they're taking Babette for a walk. I released her last night when I confirmed the claims."

I wished I could bite back tears the same way I held my tongue by keeping my fang snagged on my lower lip. Tears stung my eyes. I tried to blink them away, but it wasn't soon enough. Gratitude warmed me, and I couldn't help but throw my arms around his neck. He was only doing his job, but for some reason I wanted to thank him for checking the video again. And for stating—the whole time—that he knew Mae would never commit this crime.

With my arms high around his neck, his hands had nowhere to go but to my waist to return the hug. The gentle weight of his forearms sent heat blooming up my neck and through my cheeks. I pulled away, keenly aware of the fact that Roller Shakes was next door and Crow was Sett's neighbor. Sett and I were friends, and an intimate hug, especially while I dated Crow, was inappropriate at best.

"Mockbuster is okay?"

I nodded. "Are you going to arrest Zed?"

"I don't have enough evidence. And I don't assume. He may very well have been at Chanel's boutique that day, but it's enough to question him again—"

"I saw Reed," I blurted. Patience was never my strong suit. Sett pursed his lips, remaining silent. My weakness was his strength. He was a pillar of patience while I explained everything I witnessed.

Finishing breathless, I sucked in a whiff of Sett's scent. A mix of freshly baked bread and a drop of vanilla extract in a bottle of something stubbornly sharp like vodka. Warm despite his stone-cold skin.

"Will you stay?" he asked. He wanted me to help? This wasn't the response I expected after my lies and dangerous plan. Shock must have been evident on my face because Sett continued with an explanation of his own. "With Mayor Fitz and the deputy gone, I'm buried in work. I'd like to get this case settled soon so everyone can come home."

Emotions threatened to resurface with a sting behind my eyes.

"We've got to hurry because I promised Jovi he could bake Christmas cookies with me after you guys decided to stay in town," he said.

A little whimper escaped me, and he paused. It was all I could do not to cry again. The buildings made Bewitcher's Beach unique, but walls and bricks didn't make a home. The people did. I stayed quiet, allowing him to speak.

"Anyway, I need all the help I can get. I got a threat too. I found a note on the door at my house before the tree lighting ceremony."

"No..."

He nodded solemnly.

I lifted my chin, resolving to be...well, his *backup*. "I'll stay."

With that, Sett ducked around me and promised to return soon with both Zed and Reed. I grabbed myself a Diet Pepsi from the mini fridge and took a seat in the interrogation room—or questioning room, as Sett called it.

I hated to think of anyone as a criminal, even after witnessing Reed's vandalism with my own eyes. But someone had done it, and it felt good to get closer to answers. Closer to safety.

Warmth coated my tired limbs as I sank into the chair and replayed Sett's words in my head. Christmas cookies with the kids. Asking me to stay. *So everyone can come home.*

Diet Pepsi never tasted so good. I took another sip of the delicious breakfast and felt the caffeine already grace me with a boost of energy.

CHAPTER 19
PAINTS ON FIRE

BY THE TIME Sett had found Zed and Reed and returned to the station, the morning was a distant memory. With the hours slipping away, my morning caffeine hit had long disappeared. Now we'd been in interrogation—questioning—for the whole of the afternoon. My stomach grumbled to remind me dinner was fast approaching.

I listened to Sett's next question, ready to sniff for a truth or a lie based on the suspect's smelly emotions.

"Did you target people who protect the town because you wanted to drive us out? Or because you wanted to continue doing more damage?" he asked. After asking the basic questions, he'd gotten nothing from Zed. Everything the contractor said smelled truthful to my nose. It pushed Sett to dig deeper with trickier phrasing, and this inkling was shaped into rather genius questions. Surely, Zed would have to confess why he'd gone after us.

"I wasn't targeting anyone," Zed said, leaning forward with his elbows on the table. Reed was the opposite, sunken into his chair, chin dipped to his chest, arms folded, and with his chair pushed as far away from the table as possible.

Lavender filled the room like a meadow in spring, and I nodded at Sett to confirm the truthfulness of Zed's response. Maybe he wasn't targeting anyone specific, just hoping to do enough damage to get people to pay for expensive rebuilds.

"Level with me, Zed," Sett said, crossing his arms as if he had all the time in the world to keep the two men in this stuffy room. "Your son was witnessed in plain sight painting a target on Mockbuster before it was set on fire." It was time to reveal the evidence we had and push this discussion along.

Reed bolted up, back pin straight and fingers turning white as he gripped the edges of his chair. "What?"

Zed shot a withering look at his son. "You did what?"

Reed shrank away from his father, then coughed and cleared his throat. "I swear, I don't know anything about a fire—"

"Are you spray painting again? Reed!" Zed didn't even give him time to respond before shouting his name with enough vitriol to send *me* shrinking away. "Don't tell me you're back to vandalizing!"

"It works!" Reed squealed. Ammonia from his fear stank up the room. "Or it did in the last town—people look a little closer at their houses when they're cleaning off the paint. They want renovations, and our business was crap before this. I picked places that were already junk like that cop's dump. This fire was a coincidence, I swear. You gotta believe me." He gasped between the words that spilled out of him. I pictured the deputy's little rental unit. It was old, but I wouldn't call it a *dump*. "A little spray paint wasn't hurting anything. It was just enough for them to hire us for a new paint job, and with enough of those, we'd be swimming in cash again—"

Zed growled as if he were the werewolf in this room instead of me. He slammed a fist on the table and shifted in his seat, facing his son now like we didn't exist. "You don't care about our business. You care about getting a spoiler for that damn car of yours."

Finally, ammonia melted away, and guilt's odor wafted from Reed to mingle with Zed's smoky anger. Reed stank like fish for the shame pulled out of him by his father's words.

"Why are you so ticked off?" Reed asked. He slowly straightened, deciding to challenge his father based on the weak scent of confidence that relieved the other odors. "I didn't set any fires. You know that."

"Do I?" There was a bite to Zed's tone that pushed Reed back again. His moment of challenge was over, and he slouched, wrapping his arms around his torso for a self-hug.

While Zed dropped his head into his hands, Sett turned to me and with a low voice said, "Do you mind grabbing the ghost blade from evidence?" "Evidence" was just a closet by the little kitchen in the front of the station. Bewitcher's Beach never needed a locked storage cabinet for evidence before recent attacks. The protection spell did enough to block crime until it was stripped away. Even quieter now, he whispered. "The combination is 0528. It's in a container marked 'Arson December '97' at the center of the shelf. I'd like to see Reed's reaction to it."

I nodded and stood, slipping quietly from the room. The stale coffee in the main room smelled much better than the choking odor of Reed's guilt. I hurried to the closet and carefully spun the dial on the master lock. It was looped through a U and held the door shut with a metal slab drilled into the wall. *Zero, five, two...eight!* When it popped, I pulled the lock off and yanked the door open. The shelf was packed with general supplies, bottles of cleaner, a bag of coffee, trash bags, and a couple of clear containers on the middle shelf marked "evidence" with a small white label. Though the closet was full,

Sett had everything labeled and organized, and I easily spotted the container marked for the active investigation.

I hauled the container off the shelf and unsnapped the lid. The cigarette butt I'd found was in a sealed bag along with the lighter Sett wasn't able to pull prints from. But no black blade. No matter how much I shuffled the other items around, I couldn't find the ghost blade. Frantic now, I grabbed containers of evidence from older cases and dug around. Nothing. I pushed the coffee and Windex bottles out of the way and dropped to a crouch to check the bottom shelf.

No blade.

Sett must have misplaced it, leaving it on his desk or in a filing cabinet. Though that line of thought was hard to believe. He had scribbled handwriting, but nothing else about Sett was messy. Especially when it came to investigations.

I shoved everything back into the closet and rushed around the room, checking his desk, the drawers, the floor, even the kitchen, before bursting into the interrogation room. Zed was shaking his head at Reed, and Reed was holding back tears. The young man's eyes swam but his jaw jutted out, firm in the belief that his father's business decisions were bad.

I bent to whisper into Sett's ear. "It's gone."

His neck snapped and eyes met mine, brows angled. "It can't be."

"It's not in the container, and I can't find it anywhere in the closet or around the station. I even checked inside the microwave."

He jolted to his feet, but before he could see for himself, Zed demanded his attention. "Sheriff. What are you waiting for? Arrest my son for this vandalism and teach him the lesson he deserves." Without looking at his son, he addressed Reed, only slightly tilting his head. "Every bit of your bail is coming from your savings. That spoiler is far beyond your reach."

Sett raised his hands. "I'd like to continue the questions before that." He excused himself for a quick search that yielded no blade and then returned to questioning. We needed answers fast.

We went into another back-and-forth verbal brawl, round and round. Sett asked. Zed told the truth, and Reed quivered with nerves. My stomach growled louder than a pissed-off wolf. When smoky irritation permeated the air, I narrowed my eyes at Zed. Was his anger rising and ready to burst at Reed again?

The stinging smoke prickled in my nose and forced a cough from my dry throat. Before I could take another whiff, an alarm blared. A powerful ring deafened me as it ripped through my sharp ears. For a second, I thought I was back at the edge of Mae's property where Cliff's death had scarred the earth. Had his spirit somehow returned to haunt us all and with an ear-splitting scream?

"Fire!" Sett shouted. He bolted to his feet and yanked the door open. Smoke flooded in, and Sett waved for us to get moving as he ushered us out of interrogation. One-by-one we hurried through. I headed for the front, but flames licked and cracked near the evidence closet. Toxic air gripped my throat and sent me into a round of uncontrollable coughs. I doubled over with my hands on my knees.

Sett grabbed my arm. "The back door!" He cocked his head to the hall that led past the jail cell and toward the emergency exit.

The fire alarm blared on and on as we stumbled out the back door and away from the smoke. I gulped fresh air, sucking in desperate breaths through my scratchy throat.

Once we were all safely outside, Sett grabbed the radio from his belt and called for the fire marshal. He paced and spoke into a walkie talkie while I stood between a boiling Zed and his son.

Reed no longer smelled of ammonia. Instead, an unexpected scent of confidence crept from him. Through the smoke and briny breeze, my nose deciphered sandalwood. I shot a sideways glance and caught a little smirk curling his lips.

"See?" he said, leaning forward to catch his father's eye. "I told you I didn't set the fires."

CHAPTER 20
THE NAUGHTY LIST

THE ARSONIST WAS STILL OUT THERE.

A swell of dizziness sent my head spinning, and a knot twisted my empty stomach. Swaying, I decided if I didn't eat soon, I'd wither up and blow away in the briny wind. That Diet Pepsi breakfast was nothing but bile in my throat now.

I couldn't think like this. My stomach protested with loud groans that rivaled the white noise of the fire hose. The burning was quickly under control thanks to the fire station's quick response. The fact that this didn't occur in the middle of the night like the attack on the fire marshal's house or Mockbuster probably helped.

That, at least, was a bit of relief. But relief didn't last long as Sett stalked away to discuss the cause of the fire with the marshal. This fire confirmed what Sett had said about the targets. The arsonist wanted to hurt everyone involved in protecting Bewitcher's Beach whether through investigations, law enforcement, or temporary safety tattoos....

The deputy.

Miss Raven and Crow, who preserved spirits until they reached the afterlife.

Judy with her newly-acquired magical shields.

The coroner and the fire marshal.

Mae as the self-appointed, untrained investigative journalist with her reports in the newspaper.

Me...and now Sett.

My mind churned over the details we knew. Cigarette smoker, someone at the step aerobics class—

"I'm selling your car," Zed snapped, slicing through my thoughts as I tried to make sense of the chaos. Though Sett only warned them not to leave town, they didn't so much as leave the station. Zed lectured and Reed wavered between challenging his father and shrinking away nervously. Reed squealed. Zed shouted again. Reed groaned. The hose water gushed. The wind howled through the narrow alley between the clinic and the station. In the distance, waves crashed onto the shore and an owl hooted unnaturally loudly from the woods behind us.

It was all too much. My mind refused to work through the chaos. At least not with an empty stomach and on scant sleep.

I was sick of smoke and Reed's whiny voice. The kid was in trouble for vandalism, but this fire was proof he wasn't the arsonist. I strode away from them, abandoning the argument and approaching Sett.

"I need something to eat," I said, lightly touching his arm the same way he often got my attention.

The fire marshal tapped an investigation sheet on her clipboard and then pointed to the station. "I'm going to take note of the empty container. It was evidence for this ongoing investigation, correct?" Sett gave her a curt nod, and she strode away.

Before I could delve into a swath of mind-boggling theories, I stuck to the original plan. First, I required food. "If you need me, I'll be next door. Do you want a burger or anything?" Sett's language was food. Or cooking, at least. But I didn't cook, so the best I could offer was a greasy combo plate from Roller Shakes.

Sett shook his head and offered me a sad smile. "Thank you. But I'm going to run home after this and wash up. I'll eat one of my prepped meals so I can get back here and look for the blade."

"Do you want help?"

His jaw clenched. "As much as I'd like that, you need rest."

"I'll be fine after food, and I want to find that blade. I know you're organized, so it must have disappeared right before the fire. That's not a coincidence. They must have known you would find their fingerprints on it, which officially connects it to the fires."

Sett scrubbed his palm over his face, and exhaustion dragged at his heavy eyes. "I've been strung so thin without help..." He sighed and shook his head.

I knew what he was suggesting, but Sett never misplaced evidence. He never so much as risked adding an extra pinch of salt to a recipe.

And here I was, thinking of food again. "One burger and then I'm back to help." Before he could protest, I hurried off, leaving him to resume a discussion with the fire marshal.

Roller Shakes welcomed me with a rush of aromas that had my stomach growling so loudly I swore it rivaled the blaring music. Evening attracted a crowd of skaters who enjoyed the indoor exercise away from the chilly breeze. Whitney Houston's voice echoed from the speakers as she sang about how she'd always love "you."

After I ordered and found a seat in the busy diner, my gaze slid to the manager's door. With a mindless bite of the turkey and cranberry sandwich, I zoned and munched. The savory turkey blended perfectly with a splash of tart cranberry. I dipped the corner of the bread into a ramekin of gravy and suddenly straightened when Crow emerged.

He spotted me quickly, sensing my stare. Shoving his hands into his pockets, he dodged through the rush of customers collecting skates at the rental counter. He dropped into the seat across from me.

I swallowed a bite that was too big, forcing it down my throat before meeting his eyes. "I'm sorry for wrapping you into my lie."

He shrugged. "I've lied before."

I gave him half a joyless smile before taking a sip of water to wash the sandwich the rest of the way down. When he'd been dishonest about his Calling as a reaper, it was a lie of omission and one intended to keep him safe from a stalker. I—on the other hand—was one-sighted trying to bait the arsonist without even considering his feelings. "Still. I'm sorry."

He reached across the table to tuck a curl behind my ear. This was quickly becoming his signature move right before he smiled or... his hand snaked to the back of my neck, and I was suddenly grateful I'd just taken a swig of water. With his thumb on my cheek, he gently encouraged me closer to him and we met in a kiss. It was quick, over before I could even feel his cool lips on my hot skin, but it sent flutters through my belly all the same.

He sank back into the vinyl seat, and a smirk flickered his face. "Really. You don't need to apologize. And I should have told you I was here covering Cordelia's night shift so she could celebrate Christmas early." I hadn't even asked. Crow and I didn't need to know every detail of one another's lives. In fact, I liked the sense of adventure, the butterflies, the discovery of it all.

Relief eased the tension from my muscles, and I melted into the booth. Setting the sandwich down, I took a sharp breath and let my thoughts flow. Words stumbled over one another as I explained everything that happened since I last saw him. Reed's vandalism. The fire. Both fires...

"I knew you shouldn't have stayed at Mockbuster—"

"You don't tell me what to do," I said.

Shock sent his brows flying up and his lips parted. He was stunned into silence, and I scrambled to swallow the words back down. They'd slipped out without a thought. Had the threats dug that deeply beneath the surface? The notes were a thorn between my paws, nothing but annoying at first but then poking deeper and deeper with every step.

I'd let the arsonist get to me. I'd let Cliff get to me. Too many people were demanding I leave, or investigate or—I bit back a huff and looked up at Crow. "Sorry. Again. I haven't been this sleep deprived since the pups were toddlers. But that's not an excuse."

"Honestly, it's on me." He raked his hands through his curls and frowned. "I used to be a carefree kind of guy. I did what I wanted and went where I pleased. Now I'm bound to guide spirits. Half the time they refuse to listen even though I'm trying to help them. I find myself demanding. A lot, and I hate demanding things. I'd rather just be chill. It's totally *not* fly to boss people around."

A little laugh escaped me, and the tension in my body relaxed again. "I don't think you're using 'fly' right this time. Doesn't it mean stylish?"

"Heck if I know." He lifted one shoulder in a shrug, and his half smirk matched the lopsided look. "I told you. You're cooler than me."

I rolled my eyes, but something about what he said jogged a thought. *I told you I didn't set the fires.* Since Reed wasn't the arsonist, the criminal was still out there. Prowling Bewitcher's Beach, targeting innocent people, sabotaging homes...

"I can't stop thinking about this investigation," I said, pushing the plate away from me so I could stab the table with my finger each time I mentally ticked off a clue. "The arsonist is a smoker. They were inside the studio for the first attack. They're staying at The Oyster Inn, and they took the bait I set, which means they were definitely at the campaign speeches..." My voice trailed off. There was one more piece to the puzzle that I couldn't remember. Lack of sleep was really messing with my mind. The blade was connected, sure, but it was more than that. It was missing from evidence. *Locked* evidence.

"Curses," he said. "That speech was so motivating. Out with the old and in with the new. It inspired me to overhaul Roller Shakes with updates. It needs new paint—"

"Out with the old and in with the new," I repeated as thoughts buzzed. Thanks to a full belly, my brain was working. Almost. The phrase sparked an idea, but exhaustion had me struggling to connect the clues. The picture was right there. The puzzle was almost complete. "The arsonist targeted everyone who guards Bewitcher's Beach in one way or another. They're driving us out of town." My heart skipped, and my hand shot to my mouth. *Out with the old and in with the new.*

I'd finally found the final piece of the puzzle. Sett didn't misplace the ghost blade. It was taken by the only other person who'd know the combination to the lock on the evidence closet. The person who believed my lie about video evidence and fit every other clue. The person who was burning homes...everyone's home except Sett's. The station was targeted to retrieve the last bit of evidence, but Sett...his house was still on the chopping block. He'd received a threat.

He was the last target left.

I banged my knee on the table as I scrambled out of the booth and shot to my feet. "I know who the arsonist is."

Crow blinked up at me. "What? Who?"

"I have to go—" I slapped my palm to my chest, willing my pounding heart to calm. "I have to go to Sett's house." Horrible images flashed through my mind. Sett's modest, comfortable home ablaze, and with him inside. It left me breathless and set every nerve in my body on fire. Claws extended from my fingernails. Before I knew it, right there in the middle of Roller Shakes, my clothes fell off. My body was modestly covered in fur faster than the blink of an eye. I dropped to all fours and bolted for the door.

A million thoughts whirled through my head, but I could only focus on one. The memory of Sett trapped behind a wall of flames at the fire marshal's house.

Suddenly, I understood Crow's need to protect me because I couldn't bear the thought of Sett in danger. No matter how much Sett irritated me, I'd never stopped thinking of myself as his backup. Not truly.

CHAPTER 21
HALL OF FLAME

THE FASTER I PUSHED MYSELF, the harder my paws pounded the pavement. I'd only been to Sett's house one time when Mae threw him a housewarming party. From what I remembered, it was a typical bachelor pad except for the kitchen. He'd created the kitchen to be his sanctuary. Every cooking tool known to mankind was meticulously organized on the open shelves. To see all that incinerated to ash twisted my gut and pushed me to run until my lungs went up in flames.

I weaved through the park and darted into the neighborhood behind Bewitcher's Beach Elementary. Deep in the suburb was a one-story house with a dark blue-paneled exterior and white trim. The oldest building in the neighborhood. It didn't match the modern homes and was more charming for it, just like the rest of Bewitcher's Beach.

As soon as his home came into view at the end of a widespread court, I forced myself faster and faster. Squinting in the wind, I scanned the house for any signs of smoke and fire. The steps to the small porch sagged from years of Sett's heavy footfalls, but they weren't scorched. Not a puff of smoke or lick of flames had touched his home. Relief allowed me to suck in a breath until my gaze slid to the front window.

I skidded to a halt before leaping onto the porch and accidentally alerting those inside. Through the slit in the curtain I spotted the shine of his head. For the first time, I witnessed Mayor Fitz frown. He wore the grimace as easily as every smile he'd plastered on. It sickened me. The coward was burning our homes, destroying our lives, trying to drive us from our homes, and for what?

Silently, I placed a paw on the first step, advancing with caution.

Another object caught the glint of the kitchen light. The black blade swallowed the glow like the shine of a flashlight into the depths of the sea. Fitz's fist gripped the hilt so tightly his knuckles strained and his hand shook—but not with exhaustion. I knew that feeling, the surge of adrenaline that quivers through empowered muscles. I felt it every time I shifted from human to wolf. Mayor Fitz was stronger than ever thanks to the magic imbued in the blade he wielded.

With another step, I reached the top of the porch, where I had a better view through the window. Breath stalled in my throat and my heart dropped at the sight of Sett frozen on the other end of the weapon.

The curtain framed them, one man pinning the other with the sharp point of the black-market blade. Blood slowly soaked Sett's white T-shirt where the tip dug into his sternum.

It took everything I had not to lunge through the glass and tackle Mayor Fitz right then and there. But he was too far away from the window, and I'd have to take another step to reach him, allowing him far too much time to turn on me or worse... As soon as the window shattered, he could sink the weapon into Sett's heart. It was too risky.

"You will say nothing of this and leave town." Mayor Fitz's

voice was muffled through the closed window, but I caught every word. I lifted my ears and refused to take a breath, awaiting Sett's response. Though I knew exactly what he'd say.

"You know I can't do that."

A burst of frustration flared in my chest, but it quickly melted away. This was Sett. Annoying or not, he was more like me than I'd ever realized. Stubborn to the point of his own death.

Mayor Fitz blew out a hard breath. "It wasn't supposed to get to this, but now that you know—" He suddenly groaned. "Just like Cliff. I can't—I didn't want to hurt him either. But I knew he was poking around and we'd cross paths eventually."

"Fitz, listen to me—"

The mayor was jumpy, and Sett only triggered him further. Fitz stiffened and shoved the blade a shave deeper. A gasp slipped from me as Sett winced. When Fitz glanced over his shoulder, I ducked lower and sank into the wall under the window.

Watching wasn't going to save Sett. But I had no plan, no advantage against a man wielding a weapon more powerful than my wolf strength.

"Shut up," Mayor Fitz breathed. "Just shut up. I—I told you, I really don't want to do this, so I'm giving you one more chance to agree to run. Everyone else did what they were supposed to. They left. And when they didn't, I gave them a second chance. But you and Noema are too stupid to listen."

Out with the old, in with the new. A growl vibrated in my throat, and I couldn't help but bear my fangs in a snarl. Why did he want to replace us? And with who?

"I'm not a killer, sheriff." Mayor Fitz sounded like he was trying to convince himself, not Sett.

"Then put down the weapon and we'll talk about this." His tone pricked my heart because buried in his deep voice was a tight, breathless touch of fear. Sett was staring down his death while I huddled against a wall.

"No, no. Not until you swear you will leave. Tonight. This is a good thing." Suddenly, Mayor Fitz's attitude shifted from threatening to his usual upbeat tone. *Unsettling.* "You can work at a larger police department. Get Noema out of your hair. I know you don't want her sniffing around because if she gets too close, she'll find out about your past."

My breath hitched. *His past?* As someone without much of a past—I could only remember the last eleven years of my life—I struggled to picture Sett as anything other than the stoic guardian of Bewitcher's Beach.

I dared to peek inside again, seeing Sett's jaw clenched and his eyes dropped. *What did you do?* Now wasn't the time to speculate. Not with the blade driven deeper by Mayor Fitz's impatience. I needed a plan—like yesterday.

Mayor Fitz continued, "I know how that feels. Noema was in my way too. She never leaves her stupid shop long enough."

My surveillance. That explained why I'd received a threatening note early on but Mockbuster was only recently attacked.

I couldn't barrel through the door or break through the window. I'd alert Fitz of my presence, giving him reason to finish the job and then turn on me. But if I found a way to sneak inside and creep up behind him... The element of surprise was my only option against magical strength. First, I had to get inside.

The little house didn't have a back door from what I remembered, but it had to have an open window, or—the wildlife door! Sett knew about them because it was a part of his home. If it wasn't boarded up, I could squeeze through without Fitz seeing.

"You don't know anything about me," Sett said.

A creepy laugh bubbled out of Fitz. He was entirely too

joyful for the situation. "My guy knows everything about everyone here."

I left their voices behind and crept under the window, sneaking to the same side of the house where Judy's cottage had the Creature Cutout. Flutters erupted in my belly at the sight of the opening. Raccoon paw prints covered the muddy ground outside it, and I suppressed a smirk. Sett had been feeding—or making trades—with the local wildlife. As much as I was curious about their magic, I filed the questions away for later and ducked through the opening.

Inside the tiny laundry room, I wrinkled my nose at the odor wafting from a basket of dirty clothes.

"Did you have a partner in this?" Sett's voice filled the small home, deep and firm.

"Sheriff, it's no longer your concern who does what in Bewitcher's Beach."

Carefully, I padded from the laundry room to the living room where I had a view of Mayor Fitz's back. A modest fir tree decorated the entry space between the living room and kitchen, giving me extra coverage to stay out of Fitz's sight. The Christmas tree twinkled with white lights, and a few ornaments hung on the end of the branches. I ducked beneath a low branch and scanned the situation. A porcelain gargoyle girl with two sets of wings dangled in front of me. I peered past it and shuffled another inch closer, positioning behind Mayor Fitz.

Sett swallowed hard. "Bewitcher's Beach is always my concern. Always will be—" He stopped.

Did he notice me? He blinked but didn't shift his attention. He was pinned to the wall opposite the kitchen table. The blade dug deeper, melting through his stony skin with ease. With every wince flickering over Sett's face, I had to bite back a whimper. I sat back on my haunches, ready to leap when Mayor Fitz's arm tensed and he spoke again.

"I hate to have to do this—"

I didn't let him finish.

I lunged at him, launching off my hind legs. My forepaws found his shoulders and took him down with me. The side of his head hit the ground with a thud, and he rolled to his back as I pinned him against the floorboards. I couldn't help but bite the air inches from his nose, resisting every urge to swipe across his chest with my claws. He deserved a bloody shirt, not Sett.

The blade had clattered to the wood beside us, but when he made a desperate reach for it, Sett kicked it away. He yanked the handcuffs from his belt that was strung over a chair at the kitchen table.

Mayor Fitz threw his hands in front of his face, surrendering like the coward he was. "Noema, please!"

I growled and formed the word as best as I could around my wolf tongue. "Why?" His eyes grew huge, blinking and quivering as he stared at me. He understood me, so I barked at him again. "Why!"

"It wasn't supposed to be like this!" His voice was a tinny squeal, but the words were every bit true. Through the ammonia of his obvious fear, I smelled the lavender-scented relief that came with speaking the truth. The creep was finally confessing. "I just wanted you all to leave." I snapped at the air again, encouraging him to spill more. "Someone promised me I'd be a state senator one day. Future votes. Lots of them! All I had to do was get everyone who tracked crime out of here. But I never wanted to hurt anyone! Cliff wasn't supposed to see me, but he was always poking around at the same places I targeted. I had to prepare in case we crossed paths. I just had to..." His voice gave out as he sucked in desperate gulps of air.

It was then I realized I had my full weight on his chest, my paws bearing down on his lungs. I hopped off of him and allowed Sett to step in. He gripped Fitz's arm and yanked him to his feet.

"Fitz Feet, you're under arrest for the murder of Cliff Conflick's ghost, the attempted murder of Sett Lawrence, arson—"

Fitz hung his head, shaking it as he stared at his feet. "They promised. They promised there'd be a scapegoat witness. I thought it was Mae or that stupid builder and his stupid son. I thought..." His voice trailed.

Clearly, Fitz didn't know we'd taken Zed and Reed in for questioning or he'd never have set the station on fire. The attack on Mockbuster after Reed's spray paint made sense. They were connected all along, but Reed didn't know. Fitz was using it to cover his tracks.

"I don't know how this happened. I was supposed to be president someday. They promised..." He repeated it breathlessly. Defeated.

Sounds like some politicians lie, don't they? I bit back another bark and let Sett finish the Miranda rights while speculation swirled in my head.

Who had bribed Mayor Fitz to get rid of us? And would they come after us again?

CHAPTER 22
CHRISTMAS DAY

LEANING FORWARD, I tugged the socks higher on my ankles and then sank back into the theater chair for a better view of the arrest. This time Harry and Marv—the two bandits in *Home Alone 2: Lost in New York* were captured in Central Park after the main character got separated from his family.

Halen hopped onto his seat at the theater's front row. He mimicked the frustration on the criminals' faces, which Dio took as a challenge to out-act his brother. He mirrored Halen, who pretended to play the part of the short, bald bandit. I scooped a spoonful of chilled cranberry salad and almost choked as a laugh interrupted my swallow. Dio performed a perfect version of Marv's fear of pigeons. While the kids melted into a pile of laughter, Hattie and I exchanged knowing looks. Dio definitely deserved a role in Everland Theater's final play, before we transformed it from stage to screen.

With Mayor Fitz in jail and his campaign money donated to rebuilding the burned buildings, we finally rested easy, celebrating Christmas as it should be—with good food and better friends.

Mae pointed her fork at my bowl of fluffy pink salad and

hummed as she finished a bite. "Delicious, right? I already told Sett he owes me his secret recipe."

On my other side, Crow cocked an eyebrow. "I think he owes you a lot more than that. Arresting you was crazy."

"He was only doing his job!" I said a little too loudly.

Hattie and Sett twisted to look at me from where they hovered over a folding table full of food. Since when had I felt the need to defend Sett? Wasn't I just as irritated with him only days ago? I wiggled my bottom lip back and forth along the tip of one of my fangs, watching Sett lift a plate of creamy mashed potatoes to Hattie's nose so she could take a long whiff. She pointed at a pad of butter and instructed him to add another dollop to her "smelling plate." The entire theater was a swirl of mouth-watering aromas from the steaming honey-glazed ham to the green bean casserole and cinnamon applesauce. We had enough to feed half the town, but our close-knit crew were the only ones enjoying tonight's movie projected on the theater's curtain.

Crow sat back and followed my line of sight, glancing between me and Sett before I blinked. "At least, that's what Sett would say."

Mae dropped her voice to a conspiratorial whisper. "Well, it's certainly not the first time I've seen the inside of a jail cell. But I swore those years were behind me. I don't blame Sett." She dunked her fork into a pile of the pink salad from her own plate and lifted it high. "I'll forgive him as long as he gives up his secret ingredient." She took a bite and turned to Wallace to share the next scoop of cranberry.

Crow took a swig of eggnog and then shifted in his chair to face me. "I'm not going to question your safety again. You know what the heck you're doing."

My lips parted, and my shock and confidence made for an

odd smell. "I appreciate that." I tilted my head and mirrored his small smile.

Rarely did anyone give me the benefit of the doubt. Sett always thought he knew what was best for my safety. Mae even tried to give unsolicited advice every now and then. Hattie had her way with words, speaking bluntly when I didn't ask for her opinion.

But for a moment, I saw myself the way Crow did—capable, competent, a werewolf who could stand on her own two feet just fine. It felt pretty dang *fly*. My smile spread into a goofy grin. I grabbed my mug of apple cider and took a sip before anyone witnessed my silly expression.

Crow shook his head and tore his gaze from the movie. Dark curls fell into his eyes. "I feel like we should have known that Mayor Fitz was the creep trying to push people out of town. Nobody is that happy all the time." He mocked a dramatic full-body shudder. "Just thinking about his never-ending smile gives me the heebie-jeebies."

"He hid it pretty well with all the promises and positive talk. I just wish I understood why he did it. Why take a bribe when he had a fair chance against Dr. Pitt? The race was a hair's difference, but Fitz had experience."

Babette nearly jumped into my lap when Mae whipped around. Of course she had one ear eavesdropping. With a mischievous curl of her lip and one arched eyebrow, I knew I was about to get the answer to all of my questions. "This news isn't supposed to be released until tomorrow with the morning paper, but Fitz came out with a tell-all."

Both Crow and I scooted to the edge of our seats and gave Mae our full attention. He waved a hand to encourage her. "So are you willing to tell all today?"

"Seeing as I didn't get you a Christmas present..." She paused for dramatic effect, her red eyes twinkling at Crow. "I suppose I can give you this. Wallace was helping on the campaign to gather information for me. I'd been working on a piece for the paper for when Fitz was elected for another term as mayor. As you know, the story now has a twist. He was contacted by someone he believed was another politician. They tricked him with a promise of votes up the ladder in politics. If he sold out Bewitcher's Beach."

"Sold out?"

"Get rid of everyone in law enforcement or in the business of security here. My guess is that our precious little town here is the target of some illegal activity and this chump was playing Fitz. They probably aren't even in politics. He said he even took up smoking again from the stress of it all."

Illegal activity? Claws seemed to grip my heart and lungs. Could this same *chump* be the person who removed the protection spell? If they wanted to get away with murder, the magic had to be stripped.

Conversations and laughter muted. I only heard the thud of my pulse, pounding and offbeat in my ears.

My attention returned to the movie as Crow and Mae continued their speculations and gossip regarding Mayor Fitz. Or rather, Felon Fitz. The main character on the projected screen had found his way into a lavish hotel room decorated beautifully for the Christmas season. The image of luggage and a hotel room settled my buzzing nerves.

Now that Mockbuster was safe, at least temporarily, we could finally take that road trip. We *needed* to take that road trip. To get answers on how to secure Bewitcher's Beach again. The spell used to be a precaution, to shield the dense crowd of supernatural people here from hunters.

But the town was a target for something else now. More than ever, the spell belonged intact over Bewitcher's Beach, and we couldn't do it without help. Shadowvale University was full of experienced witches and warlocks working to study *The Book of Prophecies.*

Whoever bribed Mayor Fitz and removed the protection spell must have once had access to the grimoire. Maybe while it was hidden right here in town. If we tracked use of the magic from its spells, would we find the person attacking our home?

Join Noema for another enchanting mystery in *Banshees, Boomboxes, and Bones: Book 4 of the Bewitcher's Beach Paranormal Cozy Mysteries!*

Please consider leaving a review at your favorite place to purchase books! Also, a share with your friends who love to laugh and solve mysteries would be greatly appreciated. My quest as an author is to make others feel seen through the adventure of fiction. Please reach out to me and let me know if my stories have touched you. You, dear reader, are who this book was written for.

BEWITCHER'S BEACH
RECIPES

SETT'S CRANBERRY FLUFF

When to eat: as a sweet side to your holiday dinners. Whether you're celebrating the Ghost Pirate Moon or Christmas, cranberry fluff is a delicious complement to a savory main course. Just don't brag about the taste in front of a ghost—and be sure to let them smell it!

Ingredients:

- 3 cups of cranberries
- 2 cups of sugar
- 1 cup crushed pineapple (one 8 ounce can)
- 16 Oz(1 pint) of heavy whipping cream
- About 5 cups of mini marshmallows

Instructions:

- Mince cranberries.
- Mix all ingredients except the heavy whipping cream and refrigerate overnight.
- Whip cream into the fluff right before it's time to enjoy.
- Serve and sniff—I meant, eat!

MAE'S HOLIDAY HAM

When to eat: at a gathering or whenever you're craving a cozy meal. Did Mae steal this recipe from Sett and put her name on it? Maybe. Maybe she's still not entirely out of her thieving days. You'll never know...Unless Noema solves that mystery too.

Ingredients:

- Spiral cut ham (these are precooked)
- A spicy mustard of your choice
- Whole cloves
- 16 Oz can of sliced pineapple

Instructions:

- Rub a generous amount of spicy mustard all over ham—as much as your heart desires! Place ham in a slow cooker.
- Stab whole cloves into ham until it looks like a patchwork pattern.
- Dump sliced pineapple over ham and cook on low for 8 hours.
- Brag about how amazing it tastes, and share with friends.

NOEMA'S WARM APPLE CIDER

When to eat: whenever there's a chill in the air! If you don't cook, that's okay because neither does Noema. And here's the truth, you can select your favorite type of apple and cut, peel, core to make it more homemade. But Noema? She just picks up a bottle of apple cider from the grocery shop next to Mockbuster and customizes it. Like her, you might be too busy to go the extra 'apple'. So here's an easy recipe to cozy up with this fall!

Ingredients:

- 6 cups pasteurized apple cider
- 1 ½ cups light brown sugar
- ¼ teaspoon ground allspice
- ⅛ teaspoon ground nutmeg
- ½ teaspoon whole cloves
- 2 cinnamon sticks

- 1 orange peel

Instructions:

- Combine cider, sugar, allspice, and nutmeg in a saucepan over medium heat until sugar dissolves.
- Add cinnamon sticks, whole cloves, and the orange peel and simmer for 20 minutes.
- Strain or scoop out the sticks, cloves, and peel.
- Serve immediately, and absorb the cozy!

ABOUT THE AUTHOR

Congenital Heart Defect survivor, Emily Fluke, finds joy and peace through the expression of writing. She is a firm believer that all stories need a little magic and a lot of excitement. Emily and her husband spend their free time wrangling two children and playing video games in their busy California lifestyle. Otherwise, you'll find Emily solving an escape room, running, or writing Magic the Gathering-based poetry.

To stay up to date on new releases and connect with me, visit my website at Emilyfluke.com or follow me on social media under Author Emily Fluke, or @emilyflukefairytales.